WET SKIN

MLR PRESS AUTHORS

Featuring a roll call of some of the best writers of gay erotica and mysteries today!

Maura Anderson	Samantha Kane
Victor J. Banis	Kiernan Kelly
Jeanne Barrack	JL Langley
Laura Baumbach	Josh Lanyon
Alex Beecroft	Clare London
Sarah Black	William Maltese
Ally Blue	Gary Martine
J.P. Bowie	ZA Maxfield
P.A. Brown	Jet Mykles
James Buchanan	L. Picaro
Jordan Castillo Price	Neil Plakcy
Kirby Crow	Luisa Prieto
Dick D.	Rick R. Reed
Jason Edding	AM Riley
Angela Fiddler	George Seaton
Dakota Flint	Jardonn Smith
Kimberly Gardner	Caro Soles
Storm Grant	Richard Stevenson
Amber Green	Claire Thompson
LB Gregg	Kit Zheng
Drewey Wayne Gunn	

Check out titles, both available and forthcoming, at
www.mlrpress.com

WET SKIN

LAURA BAUMBACH
WILLIAM MALTESE

mlrpress

Published by
MLR Press, LLC
3052 Gaines Waterport Rd.
Albion, NY 14411

Visit ManLoveRomance Press, LLC on the Internet:
www.mlrpress.com

Cover Art by Deana C. Jamroz
Editing by Kris Jacen
Printed in the United States of America.

ISBN# 978-0-9793110-9-3

First Edition 2009

Slippery When Wet – Laura Baumbach.................................... *1*

The Drive Home – Laura Baumbach *27*

The Cataracts, Part One – William Maltese............................ *39*

Wet Sheets – Laura Baumbach... *91*

The Cataracts, Part Two – William Maltese *115*

Wet Dreams – Laura Baumbach.. *167*

South of the Border – Laura Baumbach................................. *175*

Slippery When Wet

Laura Baumbach

The first bead of sweat that broke loose ran from the man's temple to the sharp angle of his tight, square jaw. It hung on for an anxious moment, during which Parker realized he had been holding his breath, waiting to see where the bead would land on the solid expanse of bulging hard muscle that formed the casually spread, naked thighs beneath it.

Eyes hungry, Parker hoped it would splash high on the man's leg, giving him a reason to follow its descent. He didn't actually need a reason, it was a public sauna. An on site, twenty-four hour, fully outfitted gym, pool and sauna, a perk of working for a huge corporation that promoted employee health and fitness.

But Parker still insisted on playing this game with himself. Seeing how much restraint he could muster, how long he could hold back his physical desires without the other guy suspecting. What it would take to make him finally get up and leave, towel artfully wrapped around his hips while his hands covered his growing erection. Then a warm shower to cover the quick hand job before he toweled off, dressed and made his way alone back to his peaceful but empty apartment.

Working sixteen hours days was great for his work and reputation as a dedicated researcher for the company. Not so great for his personal life. If he thought about it, his current lifestyle of nothing but work and sleep was pretty pathetic for twenty-nine year old, moderately successful forensic scientist. So he didn't spend much time thinking about it.

And there was no time to look for dating material outside his immediate circle. All of his close associates were either female or straight men. There wasn't anyone he was interested in anyway. Or there hadn't been until three weeks ago when Sir Brawny & Buff started showing up in the gym every night. Parker had nearly dropped a free weight on his foot the first time B&B had strode into the gym and began his warm up. By the time the other man had ended his routine almost two hours later, Parker had hit the head twice to jack off. Which was the only reason he'd managed to stay in the sauna with the guy for six whole minutes before leaving weak kneed and dizzy, still half hard and aching.

It didn't help any that they were always alone, the last hardcore exercise junkies in the place. Or the only people that worked long hours into the evening and still had energy to burn. Parker worked out so his body would be exhausted enough that his mind would have to shut off to sleep. He was toned and wiry, but his short, slender frame would never compete with this guy. B&B was all muscle. Muscle, muscle everywhere.

But there might as well have been a big neon 'do not disturb' sign tattooed on the guy's chest. They had been alone together working out in the gym five and six nights a week for two hours and the guy had yet to do more than stare Parker in the eye for ten seconds and nod a wordless hello. Talk about your strong silent type!

Of course, Parker hadn't offered any attempts at conversation either. He'd been content to ogle covertly and fantasize. No one else in the gym meant privacy, but it also meant no witnesses to murder if the guy took offense to Parker's... appreciative interest. But then the guy would actually have to notice before he could be offended and Parker made sure that wasn't going to happen. *No way.* He wanted to see his next few birthdays.

Licking his lips, Parker tasted the sharp tang of his own sweat. He closed his eyes and let his muscles relax, feeling the knots in his neck and shoulders from hunching over microscopes and keyboards all day start to unwind. This was always the perfect ending to his day, the way he unwound, the only activity truly draining enough to shut down his mind *and* body. Besides sex. And sex was nowhere on the immediate horizon. One handed sex didn't count. It was rewarding but not exhausting.

The sauna was big enough for ten people, all wooden slant flooring and two tiered benches. In the center of the room was a small sculptured pedestal filled with steaming hot rocks. A tiny basin that filled with water automatically was artfully designed into one side and a ladle hung from a part of the sculpture.

The sudden hiss of water hitting hot stones filled the air. Startled, Parker looked up under half-closed eyelids to watch B&B replace the ladle, towel slung low around solid, molded-from-rock hips and ass. So low and loosely wrapped that when B&B stepped away the towel slipped. B&B casually grabbed one end of it and instead of re-wrapping it, threw the towel over his broad and brawny shoulder.

Full frontal exposure. No steroid user here! It was just like Christmas. And man, would Parker like to play with that toy! Christ, this guy was one complete package. Too bad he didn't have a personality to go with the body.

Parker's breath caught in his throat. He prayed the grunt of appreciation that escaped couldn't be heard over the hiss of the steam.

The guy radiated power, even an element of danger. Parker found that thrilling, different. He'd never been attracted to guys like this before, but then he'd never socialized in circles outside of academia and scientific research. He found it amazing a guy like this was in the same workplace as he was. He knew the guy worked there, he'd seen one of the female techs trying to chat him up in the hallway yesterday. Parker had panicked at the thought of having a conversation with the guy outside the isolated exercise wing. He'd walked right by, avoiding eye contact, blood rushing in his ears too loudly for him to catch any of the conversation between the other two.

What did Broad & Brawny do here? Security? Not likely. He was too controlled, too deliberate. This guy's whole demeanor screamed intelligence and stealth with a good dash of lethal force thrown in for good measure, at least in Parker's lively imagination. A bodyguard for one of the head honchos maybe?

Parker shook his head. He was spending too much time looking at the world at a microscopic level. But man, he would like to get a closer look at this guy, a much closer look.

Every muscle group on the man's body was developed to perfection, and not from just working out in any gym. Parker could see scars on his barrel chest, back, and his beefy left arm. They didn't look like they came from any surgeon's scalpel. A long, jagged, barely healed scar decorated his now bare right hip. Hips that were leaner than his wide, swaying shoulders with gluts rippling with constrained power as the man walked.

Parker knew this because, instead of returning to his old seat on the bench across the room, B&B was walking toward Parker. Slow and deliberate. Was that a little swagger in those rock formations other people called hips and thighs?

The appreciative grunt turned into a strangled cough at the back of Parker's throat. The swagger was slight, but since it made the stiff, gloriously jutting erection sprouting up from the dark nest of hair bob and sway, Parker couldn't help but notice—the tiny swagger *and* the not so tiny hard-on. Not anywhere *near* tiny.

He swallowed past the sudden constriction in his throat and concentrated on dragging his gaze away from the flushed and gleaming circumcised shaft before he drooled on himself.

Self-consciously, he crunched his own towel into a concealing ball in his lap. As his gaze pulled away, he'd meant to look at the ceiling, but some alien magnetic force invaded the room and forced what he knew was a wide-eyed stared to meet the man's gray-blue gaze.

Steely gray looked less… well… steely up close. More blue, with a glint of humor and a splash of something Parker would have called interest in someone else. And was that the beginnings of a sneer or… a smile on those firm, sweat moistened lips?

Without a word, Broad & Brawny dropped to the bench beside Parker, cock at full mast, proudly on display. B&B leaned back against the wall and got comfortable. His towel became a pile of crumpled fabric on the floor. A slick hard knee bumped Parker's thigh but he was too busy trying not to stare to react to the touch.

"Hey." The voice was a little softer than expected, masculine but with a smoothing timber to it. It lessened some of Parker's trepidation. "Name's Dallas."

A large, smooth hand crossed over Parker's lap, fingers spread and grip waiting perilously close to Parker's own stiff soldier. He automatically reached out and shook hands. The heat of the guy's skin was like Parker imagined it would be picking up one of the steaming sauna rocks, slick with penetrating warmth that was almost a living entity on its own.

"Ah… hi." His voice was raspy, partly from the thick air clogging his lungs and partly from surprise.

"Come here often?" The tone was light but the laser blue stare demanded an answer.

"Huh?" Parker blinked, uncertain what he should say. He decided to play it safe. "Ah, every night, same as you."

The small smile spread into a dazzling grin. Dallas leaned his head and shoulders down closer to Parker and gently added, "It was a joke. You know, lighten the mood, break the ice. A come on line."

"Oh. Sorry. I don't… go out much." Sudden he felt like he was back in high school. "Not recently." How much of dork did that make him sound like. "Not like *never*… just not… recently." *Oh, yeah, that was soooo much better.*

"Tina says you work about 90 hours a week. Hard to work in a social life with those hours. Hell, it has to be hard to work in sleep and food with those hours."

"Tina?" Trying to ignore the sweet, staggering sight of a bead of creamy white sitting on the dusky pink crown of the thick cock only inches away, Parker fixated on the part of the conversation he didn't already know all about.

"Yeah. Says she's known you for three years? The little blond I was talking with when you breezed by me in the hallway yesterday afternoon?"

"Oh, yeah." Parker stammered and tore his gaze away, fighting the urge to lick his lips. "Sorry." The image of Dallas' cock pressed to his lips clouded his mind. He was woefully aware he sounded as if his IQ had dropped fifty points. "Tina works in testing."

Parker looked at his own lap. Fisted white knuckles wrapped in the towel stared back at him like little glassy eyed aliens. This whole conversation belonged on another planet. Surreal and bizarre.

"Testing's not my field of interest."

"So she said." In the silence that followed, Parker squirmed, trying to relax. He shot a glance at his companion to find Dallas studying his face, a thoughtful, tentative look on his rugged features and a flash of something indefinable in his eyes.

Parker felt a slight tightness in his chest. Lord, was this guy coming on to him? He hated being scrutinized, evaluated. If it involved anything other than his intellect, he always felt as if he came up short. Especially when the person doing the physical scrutinizing was bigger, broader, beefier, and better looking. Not that he was skinny or ugly; he worked out every night, but mostly cardio training, not to put on bulk or build muscles like this guy sported. Parker liked to think of himself as small but wiry.

The faint smile was back on the big man's handsome face. It tugged one corner of his mouth higher than the other, bringing a dimple to life in one cheek. Parker realized a faint white line on the upper lip was an old scar, deep through the vermilion border of Dallas' lip. What had hit him so hard his face had been split wide open? And why?

"She had a lot to say about a lot of things." There was a flash of humor in that. Unexpected, revealing a glimmer of the man Parker hadn't anticipated.

Dallas rolled his shoulders. Parker could hear his spine flex and pop. He wondered if all that power and strength came out when the guy was in bed. That proud weapon standing up saluting between his legs was like a freaking light saber, long thick and no doubt deadly. Parker had to swallow hard to keep his throat from closing up.

"But we weren't talking about work."

"No?" It was almost a whisper. He wondered where this conversation was going but at the same time, almost afraid to find out.

"I think she was trying to wheedle a date out of me."

"Oh…" *Bingo. The guy wanted info on Tina. That's what this was about. Damn it.* "She's… pretty."

And folks, this is why fantasies are called fantasies. They never become reality. So much for the imagined sauna blow job.

"A little over enthusiastic maybe, but… nice." He studied the folds of the towel in his lap again. Pretty soon he wouldn't need it to cover anything more shocking than a limp cock. "And… and pretty."

"Pretty is nice." Dallas didn't seem to notice Parker's discomfort and lackluster disinterest. "She talks a blue streak though."

"Yeah." He took a deep breath and wiped a trickle of sweat of his upper lip. He darted a look to his left, catching that small, slightly asymmetrical smile again. Those dark eyes really should stop staring at him with that warm, intoxicating glint. "I-I like… quieter people."

"She's not really my type either."

He chanced another glance. Yep, that warm, 'I'm looking at *you*' stare was still in the guy's eyes. Parker ran his tongue along his lower lip, then stopped when Dallas gaze dropped to follow the movement then returned to study Parker's face. "You like them quieter, too?"

"Um-um." Gaze pinning Parker in place, Dallas made a nondescript wave in the air that conveyed nothing.

The words tumble out before Parker could stop them. "You like them *uglier*?"

There was short, stunned silence than a pleasant rumble of laughter shook the bench. Dallas' upper arm rubbed against him, transmitting the vibrations so their skin touched in a thin layer of combined sweat. It felt like static electricity crackled between them, making Parker's arm tingle.

"No." Dallas shook his head once, the sweat trickling off his angular jaw to splash on his chest, disappearing in the patches of dark chest hair. "Holy Christ." It was said softly, low, disbelieving, but Parker heard it and flinched. Was he that much of a dork to this guy? "Not uglier." His gaze searched Parker's face for a moment, their arms still touching. The warmth of the room was suddenly suffocating as Parker imagined he saw more than idle curiosity burning in Dallas' intense stare. "I just like my dates to be more... male."

"Male? You?" He was surprised by how husky and low his voice sounded. Interested, maybe even... sexy. His cock was sure interested. It poked at the towel, straining the fabric, nudging Parker's hand, looking for escape. "As in *men*?" His gaze locked on Dallas' steady stare, wanting to look away but afraid if he did he'd misread what he was hearing.

"That's the best kind of 'male' I can think of, yeah." Both the answer and the stare held steady, an invisible thread holding Parker captive.

"You're gay?" It was still a little hard to wrap his mind around. Sure he knew there were gay men that were walking talking hunks with perfect brawny bodies and chiseled good looks, but Parker thought all of them were in porn flicks. He knew he'd never met one. Until apparently now.

Dallas nodded and that tolerant smile grew a little bigger than before. "I think I just said that."

"*You* date men?"

"Good lord. You need to get out of the laboratory more, Dr. Crowe. Do you talk to anyone in the world outside these walls?"

Ignoring the sarcasm, Parker shifted in the attempt to cover the stirrings of renewed interest under his own towel. "You know my name?"

"I asked Tina who you were when you walked by—without even a hello. She and I were doing something unusual. You might try it sometime. It's called social interaction. You seriously need to polish up your skills."

He leaned forward, elbows on his knees, his cock pressing straight up to touch his abdomen. But his eyes still studied Parker. The interest was still there but muted as he recited his newfound information as if he was reading a report out loud.

"Dr. Parker Crowe, a certified genius with four degrees specializing in the field of chemistry and biophysics. A valued, dedicated scientist in the company's esteemed R&D laboratory. Dedicated to the point of ridiculousness. Working late into the night, every night, plus most weekends. Unlike Tina, I don't see that as a bad thing, mostly. I respect hard work." The formal, harder edge that had crept into his voice slipped away and the interest was back full force. "But you have to balance it with a life on the side." Dallas reached out and ran the back of one hand down Parker's smooth, sweat-slick chest.

"Why?" The light touch made his nipples harden and his swollen, trapped cock ache for attention, but Parker couldn't help it, curiosity always won out over… everything. It a single-mindedness that made him good at this job, but it had derailed many an intimate moment as well.

"Why what?" Now it was Dallas' turn to sound confused. "Why do I respect your dedication?"

"No, why did you ask who I was?"

"Okay. Looks like we do this the hard way." The snort spoke volumes of restrained tolerance with a large dash of exasperation. "Look, the long version is we've been working out together for three weeks without a word between us. The short version is… I'm attracted to you. Wanted some personal info on you before I made a move."

"Worried I'd be offended if you came onto me?"

"The way you've been checking me out since day one?" Dallas made that amused grunted again. "I knew you were interested."

"Uh?"

"Face it, Doc. You aren't very good at sneaking looks."

Darting his gaze away from Dallas' crotch, Parker squirmed. Dallas teasingly confided, "You'd make a lousy stalker, Doc."

"Yeah, well… you still haven't answered why?"

"Wanted to know if you were seeing anyone. Don't need a jealous boyfriend cropping up somewhere down the line. Don't need extra drama in my life. My job gives me plenty."

"Job?" He couldn't keep his eyes off Dallas' cock. It was delicious looking, slightly curved, long in the shaft with veins that looked like ropes dangling from the circumcised crown. It thickened at the base just before disappearing into a forest of dark curls.

"Christ. Yeah, my job. That thing I do during the hours I'm not asleep or working out with you." Dallas slid off the bench and crouched by Parker's knee. His cock lay flat on his sculptured abdomen, a stark smooth pole against the tanned flesh and dark hair.

"Security?"

"Kind of, but not really."

"Then what are you?" His knees were nudged further a part, empty space replaced with broad shoulders connected to a solid mass of muscle and heat. Hands massaged his thighs, the grip firm with steady pressure that transmitted power.

"Besides a guy with a monster hard-on sitting next to the attractive guy that gave me the boner? The guy with a woody just as hard as mine?" Dallas slowly but firmly pulled Parker's towel away from his lap to let it join the other discarded towel at their feet. Parker let it slip away. "Is it important right now?"

"Ah... ah."

Warm, firm lips slipped over the tip of Parker's cock. He shuddered, gasped, and fought the urge to clamp his legs together from the sudden shock. Not that he could have closed them, not with the tree-trunk-solid torso between his knees, leaning into his body, forcing him to lie back, relax and accept. "Holy crap."

Lips traveled over the head and down one side, returning to the crown again and again, firm, moist and hungry. Ribbons of saliva mixed with sweat glistened on the dusky pink shaft.

The steam laden air filled his lungs, each gasped breath seemingly filled with less oxygen than the one before it. Mammoth hands under his ass lifted his weight, coaxing his hips to the edge of the bench. Parker blindly obeyed.

He was rewarded by having his cock engulfed in a hot sleeve of slick flesh. Dallas worked the shaft with the rough flat of his tongue. Then he applied pressure to the underside of the swollen head with the firm, pointed tip before deep-throating the newly sensitized rod.

Suction pulled Parker's cock in until he could feel the tight ring of lips pressed up against his body. Grunted puffs of hot breath emanated from Dallas' nose buried in his groin hair. The suction under his taut sac tugged on the root of his cock. The rhythm pulled and released, teasing the muscles in his perineum. His asshole clenched and spasmed, eager to become part of the action. Fingers brushed his hole then dug into his ass and pulled him closer.

"Holy—!" Parker couldn't remember the last time he'd had sex with a partner this satisfyingly aggressive. Or this sexy.

Sensation overwhelmed reason, want pushed aside his natural awkwardness, and lust granted his newfound, if temporary, lover a measure of trust he wouldn't have given easily under other circumstances. He needed to relax and enjoy it. Like, really. This *didn't* happen every day.

Who was he kidding? He was a scientist. His life didn't include impulsive, covert sex in the company sauna. Or anywhere else for that matter. This *couldn't* be happening.

Yet, here he was. Getting an outstanding blowjob from an assertive hunk who was, realistically, a complete stranger.

The heat in the room leveled off. The steam dissipated but the air hung humid and heavy, coating both their bodies in rivers of sweat.

The hands holding his hips immobile slipped. Their grip instantly repositioned. One arm slid behind his low back to drag him forward a few more inches, pushing his cock deeper into the mouth devouring it. He could feel fingertips branding their mark into his flank, the massaging pressure bruising but oddly comforting, a wordless reassurance this contact was more than about sex, their owner saying with a touch he was focused on Parker not just his cock.

Dallas' other hand slid up Parker's chest, palm flat against his skin like a surfboard skimming the rivers of sweat, riding the waves of rib and lean muscle. Quick, kneading fingers latched onto one nipple, plucking it over and over until it was hard, hot and swollen. Every twist and flick of the tiny nub sent flashes of burning pain to his cock, a fire that turned into an anxious glow of almost desperate pleasure. God, it had been too long.

The start of an orgasm clenched in his balls, his ass tightening, his cock swelling. His mind reeled at the sight of Dallas kneeling between his widespread legs, face buried at his groin, lips locked around his cock. The sucking increasing as if Dallas was determined to draw his climax out by sheer physical force. The mental picture of his cum shooting out to slide down Dallas' tight, hungry throat was all he needed to fall over the edge.

And that's when panic set in.

Reason suddenly intruded on the moment. "No! No, wait. Move! You shouldn't... you don't know if... Holy SHIT!" Parker pushed at the bobbing head but Dallas refused to relinquish his prize. And then it was too late.

A burst of bright lights and searing pleasure rocketed through his cock and invaded every one of his nerve fibers. The eruption was so intense his imagination, ever the scientist, turned his cum into liquid nitrogen and his climax into an atomic mushroom cloud.

He felt shell-shocked. Numb limbs sizzled, his muscles too weak to move. All he could do was lie like the puddle of sweat under his ass, limp and fluid, forced to enjoy the exquisite delights of being sucked dry and licked clean.

"Holy cow. Just—holyyy!" His voiced sounded as weak as his limbs.

A swift, stunning yank on his waist pulled him off the bench. Parker landed with a low grunt, a leg on either side of Dallas' firm lap, a stiff, leaking cock smashed against his own still half-hard, but fading fast dick.

Even as high as he was on Dallas' thighs, Parker still had to glance up to look directly into the man's eyes. Blue eyes stared back at him, so close he had to concentrate on not going cross-eyed while he held the gaze.

"Listen, I'm sorry. I-I tried to warn you." Parker hands instinctively moved to Dallas' wide shoulders. He used the solid wall of flesh to push his torso back a few inches, gaining mental distance more than any actual physical retreat. His back hit the bench behind him, but hands gripped tighter to his waist, preventing him from moving again. Panic surged. "I swear, you'll be okay. I'm healthy, I swear."

He eyes did cross as Dallas closed the gap between them, leaning in to nuzzle and nip at the tender skin at Parker's neck. "I know." A sudden lick and exaggerated kiss had Parker pushing into the contact. "I'm not worried."

"You know? How did—? You got access to my employee files?"

A sharp bite made him flinch. Dallas soothed the pain away with small kisses that skimmed along Parker's skin all the way up to his ear. A tingle of excitement flew along his nerves and his cock stirred. "I should be mad." He swallowed hard and turned his head to give Dallas more access. "But under the circumstances I'd be an idiot to object."

"And we both know you're a genius, so let's not worry about it."

Hot, wet lips massaged the lobe of one ear before it was sucked on briefly. Hands explored his chest and back, then both slid down his ass to fondle his cheeks, fingers kneading and spreading the small globes like bread dough.

"Listen, doc. I figure we've got about three minutes before one or both of us passes out from the heat in here. Let's finish off this last soldier."

Air felt as if it had just fully returned to his sluggish lungs, but Parker couldn't find the energy to speak. He merely nodded, wondering how he was going to return the blowjob in his present position.

Dallas's commanding hands urged him to move, but not in the direction he anticipated.

"Turn over. On your knees, chest on the bench."

He was gently flipped and maneuvered into place. Any thoughts of protest got lost in the excitement of how inappropriate their behavior was. Parker grabbed the edge of the bench and rested his cheek on the smooth wood under his chest and face. His legs were still spread, stretched wide to bracket Dallas's lower body, rising cock and loose balls swinging free in the space created below his lower belly. He was completely exposed, open to anything the other man wanted, and barely able to tolerate the wait to find out what that was.

"Yeah, just like that. Let me see that tight, little ass of yours."

Hands ran the length of his back, rubbing his skin, the touch heavy, firm, reassuring. The hair of Dallas's thighs and groin scratched against Parker's legs and ass, then the heat of flesh pressed more fully against him, weighing him down. He felt blanketed by Dallas's body, covered from neck to knee in body heat. Skin on skin. Too much skin! This was going too far. Parker had never let sexual excitement over rule reason when his health was concerned.

"No! We can't. I don't... we don't have a condom. I won't—" He pushed up, but barely managed to raise more than a few inches. His lack of success had nothing to do with the strong arm on his back and everything to do with his limp and uncooperative limbs. In fact, Dallas rolled him a little onto his side and leaned in close to reassure him, understanding in the eyes under the lusty waggle of dark eyebrows.

"Relax, professor. We aren't going to. I'm clean, but I don't expect you to take my word for it." A rough tussle of his hair ended on a slow trail of fingers down his spine. It was seductive, coaxing. He was eased back on his stomach again. "Right now—just trust me."

"What—"

"Relax. Trust me." Lips kissed down the path the fingertips had blazed on his skin. One cheek was gripped, his opening exposed. One rough swipe of a towel dried off his skin, teasing his asshole, making it wink and clench. "I've got this one covered."

The lips moved lower, not wasting time. Dallas's tongue darted out to lavish broad, wet laps over Parker's ass, then moved rapidly into the sensitive cleft. There it wiggled and stroked until it wormed its way to the puckered entrance. Once there the broad strokes vanished, replaced by a firm penetration that darted in and out of his body in a breathtakingly fast tempo. His heart matched the beat, his cock filling with each pounding note, his lungs struggling to keep up.

Parker gasped and tried not to move. He wasn't a virgin, but this was more than any of his previous fumbling, awkward lovers had tried in the past. This felt better than anything he had ever experienced before, mind blowing, thought destroying and completely amazing.

Then things got even better.

Suddenly the tongue disappeared. An insistent pressure breached his opening, filling him with something thicker, but still slick and warm, alive. The remaining brains cells not consumed by lust recognized it as a finger, long and dexterous. It stretched the ring of muscles at his opening, making them tingle with a delicious burn. A steady downward pressure and the digit pressed deeper into his channel, rubbing, curling, reaching until it bumped his prostate. His limbs stiffened and trembled, the lancing shock of electric stimulation lighting up his nerves.

He could feel Dallas's groin rubbing against his ass while strong palms manhandled his thighs together, the man's poker hot shaft trapped between them.

"That's it. Squeeze tight." Hot, muscular flesh smacked against the outside of Parker's quivering thighs, clamping them together like a vise. "Ah, yeah, just like that." Dallas leaned over him, his weight snug to Parker's back, one arm curled around Parker's waist to grab hold of Parker's straining dick.

"I'll do all the work." The cock slid deeper then out, the smooth silky glide of sweaty flesh on slippery flesh. "You just think about my hand up you tight little hole. Fingering you.

Tickling that little cherry inside you. Think about that burn in your ass." The finger inside him stroked the swollen nub. Parker jumped, grunted and then moaned into the wood bench. "Think about what it looks like to come all over my hand."

Gripping the bench to keep from banging his head, Parker did what he was told, envisioning his cum spurting out into Dallas's massive hand, the creamy white juices stark against the tanned skin. He clenched his legs, thrilled when a gasp of pleasure hissed across his back.

"Goddamn, baby! Oh, yeah, that's my man." The strained, throaty tone made Parker's passion swell higher.

The sudden clarity that this powerful man had sought him out, checked him out and then chosen to fall to his knees just to please Parker was tremendously exciting. Parker's past sexual partners had been all equally matched with Parker in physical size and limited experience. As far as Parker was concerned this interlude was a once in a lifetime experience. He intended to enjoy every fleeting, sweaty second of it.

Flexing his spine, Parker pushed back into the wall of humping muscle pressed to his ass, primarily to enjoy the solid weight. He forced his legs a millimeter apart just to feel the power in the immediate resistance as Dallas pressed them back together again with his own thighs. He returned the pressure again, and was rewarded by the arm around his waist cinching closer. The fingers at his waist curling into his flesh in a possessive hold, reminding him there was a man attached to the cock slithering along the rarely touched regions of his ass, sliding under his balls and stroking alongside the stocky root of his own swollen cock.

Inspired, he wormed a hand down under his balls and managed to grab the head of Dallas's cock as it slid forward. He pinched the spongy tip, rubbing his fingertip around the crown's edge, teasing the flesh while the head twisted into the flat of his slick hot palm.

"Fuck, that's good!" Dallas grunted his surprise even while thrusting his hips harder to accommodate Parker's limited reach.

He'd never fucked like this, never imagined it was possible for such a benign position to give so much pleasure. It was unusual and bizarre, making it exotic and unique to Parker, heightening the thrill of 'fucking' with a total stranger in a forbidden location. The mental picture of what they must look like crouched over a bench, drenched in sweat, fucking like dogs in heat was almost enough to send him out of control. Dallas's hands beat out a sensual rhythm on Parker's body— one wrapped around Parker's cock, one hand shoved deep inside exploring his ass, massaging that sweet spot again and again.

Then Dallas added that last bit of stimulation Parker needed to make the vision complete. "Ah, baby, gotta pluck that cherry right off the branch for you."

The finger in his ass poked deeper and twisted, the tip flicking the nub inside, the callused pad swirled over the hardening kernel, each bold stroke sending flashes of intense heat coursing through Parker's shuddering body.

"Gonna make that sweet cherry mine, doc." There was a harsh grunt and the plumping motion between his legs increased, friction building. "Make you come. Make you *mine*." Dallas went stiff, frozen in place for a brief moment, then he began a frenzied pumping that would have jarred Parker's ribs across the bench if a protective arm wasn't taking the brunt of the action.

The movement forced the finger inside Parker's channel to press down, stretching his asshole and igniting the burn as it curled, adding weight to its maddening rub.

Parker couldn't tell if it was the penetration in his ass, the luscious tug-pull-twist on his dick, or the throaty, passionate groans and claiming words mumbled against his skin, or the combination of all them, but he came, hard and fast.

"Oh, god, oh god, oh god!" Small spurts of cum pumped out his slit in thick pulses he could feel shooting up his shaft. At the same moment wet, sticky heat bathed his legs and balls. Dallas's cum rubbed into his skin as he filled the other man's hand.

The slap of wet skin on wet skin was audible, but muffled. Breathing became difficult but Parker ignored it. He groaned and spurted once more, spent but still tingling with the afterglow of a great orgasm, the best one he'd had in a long time. His eager cock held out for more, barely shrinking to a stubborn half-mast.

The weight on his back and thighs suddenly eased off. He expected to be left lying alone to regain his breath, but the restraining arm still around his waist was joined by another arm, pulling him off the bench and back to rest against a heaving chest.

"That, my dear doctor, was a hell of a ride." A quick kiss branded his neck then he was being pulled to his feet by insistent arms. "Need a shower and some cooler air. Then maybe, *maybe* we'll both survive. Come on."

Parker didn't think he could talk let alone walk but Dallas wouldn't take no for an answer. He had him on his feet, stumbling out the door quicker than Parker thought was humanly possible. The man had the constitution and strength of an ox. Parker felt like a marionette with no strings attached, weak and uncoordinated.

The room spun and tilted forty-five degrees, but Parker managed to keep on his feet all the way to the deserted showers. True, the tree limb wrapped around his waist helped, but he was certain his own desire not to be found naked and dead inside the corporate headquarters private steam room motivated him just as much. Vaguely he wondered why his logical, analytical mind accepted being found naked and dead in the shower as more of a natural event, but the rush of cool air that hit him just outside the sauna stole his thoughts.

He wasn't positive, but the fact that the next thing he remembered was the spray of cool water bubbling through his hair and down his neck made him suspect he'd blacked out for a moment. He became conscious of hands briskly scrubbing his legs, his back plastered to the cool tile of the shower wall, his weight held in place by a widespread palm on his sternum. Looking down, he could see only a dark head set on broad shoulders kneeling in front of him.

"Hey." It was weak and more mumble than he had hoped, but it was the all he could think of in the situation. He couldn't remember the man's name. And damned if his cock didn't see it as an opportunity to extend itself in welcome, as well. The dark head tilted and blue gray eyes smiled up at him. Dallas. Now it was coming back to him. The perfect name for a man as big as the state of Texas. "Dallas."

"Hey, back at you, doc." The smile extended to the man's full mouth, the perfect white teeth bright against the tan skin. "You should lean back there and take a minute. I don't think you've gotten your land legs."

Dallas stood, their groins touching, his hand still planted on Parker's chest. Parker could feel his heart pounding against the restraining palm.

"I think..." dark eyes watched him, their pupils dilated, a gleam of satisfaction in them coming closer and closer as Dallas narrowed the distance between their faces, open mouth hovering just above Parker's nervously twitching lips. Water hit Dallas's back, shielding Parker from the wide spray. "I think I... lost a little time between the sauna and here."

"Just a little." That wicked smile split Dallas's face. "It was cute."

"Cute?" As weak as he was, he still thought he managed to convey all the righteous indignation the comment deserved. He was a grown, albeit slight, man, and a respected scientist, a noted professional! He was not *cute*!

The palm slid up around his neck and into his hair. Dallas's hefty weight held him up and pinned him to the wall. The scent of sex and soap clung to Dallas despite the shower spray. Parker could smell his own cum on Dallas's breath, warm, musky, and damn it, he wanted to taste it, to know for himself what it was to savor himself on the big man's tongue. Even now, his gaze was glued to those dusky pink lips, drinking in the sounds they made, willing them to come closer. They quirked in another of those blinding, cocky, delighted smiles.

"Oh, yeah. All kind of confused and helpless." The lips came nearer. Not because Dallas had moved, but because he'd tugged Parker's head closer by his hair. "Like I said—cute."

Dark eyes studied his face. Parker's cock hardened to full length, slipping upward to poke into Dallas's balls. A quick shift of the big man's hips and they were suddenly cock to swollen cock.

Parker gasped, his sigh swallowed up by Dallas's hovering mouth. "I do like cute, professor. And helpless has its appeal." A light kiss touched one corner of Parker's mouth then the other. "That is, if I'm the one making you helpless."

He could feel Dallas's heartbeat echoing through his chest, a slow, powerful hammering pulse easily half Parker's current thundering rate. Parker felt like his own muscles were made of putty. Reluctantly, he had a twinge of appreciation for big guy's bear-like burliness preventing him from collapsing to the shower floor. He was surrounded by heat and muscle and strength, a blanket of flesh, also like a shield.

He must be used to toting dead weights around. He has all those muscles for some reason, right?

This guy was pure stamina. Probably all brawn and not much brain. Probably. Not that it mattered right now. He had developed a certain appreciation for the man's... brawn, but he did have a reputation to salvage here.

"Helpless? I'm not helpless. Or confused!" A massive hand cupped his ass and ground his leaking cock into the solid flesh of Dallas's groin. Cocks slid shaft to shaft, the tip of Parker's dick bumping slick skin and coarse, grating hair. The contrast of sensations was enough to jerk his hips in a desperate effort of their own to increase the contact. Grinding his cock into Dallas stole some of the authority from his grunted claim. "I'm—I'm not helpless!"

"It would be more convincing if you didn't say it like it was a question. But that's cute, too."

"I don't get confused!"

A light kiss landed on his chin and Parker found himself angling his face to encourage the lips to hit a better target. If there was one thing Parker did know how to do it was kiss. It was the foreplay he enjoyed the most and the thing many of his sexual partners wanted to do the least.

"Okay then. Disoriented. Discombobulated. *Fucked stupid.* Pick one you like best, doc." The hand in his hair grabbed the back of his head and tilted his face up sharply. Warm breath brushed his chin, then Dallas licked the underside, slow and rough, ending with a kiss to either side of Parker's quivering jaw.

A low, raw voice whispered in his ear. "While you're deciding on that, I'm going to pick something *I* like best."

Parker opened his mouth to object. Warm lips sealed over his protest and a tongue slipped between his lips. It teased the tender lining of his lower lip, the electric touch firm and wet. It licked his upper lip, then slid between his still parted teeth, exploring, tasting, moving to map the roof of his mouth. He couldn't hold back a moan, the sound vibrating in his throat, encouraging the invasion. His tongue battled with Dallas's and they fell into a rhythm of stroke and rub, their hips mimicking the dance, cocks and tongues dueling, sliding, grinding against each other, neither looking for dominance, happy with an equal play of give and receive.

Parker lost himself in the kiss—the subtle exchange of power, the tender caress of lips, the gentle sucking of his tongue, the wet warmth that reminded him he was in the arms of a man who seemed to value him for something other than his brains or his corporate position. Dallas had taken the time to learn about him, not just his intimidating elevated IQ or his high security, high paying job, but about *him.* And miraculously, the man had looked past all of the things that usually turned off all but the most scientific minded of potential lovers. Dallas seemed amused by Parker's lack of social skills and obvious inexperience, possibly even… attracted by them. It was apparent the man was definitely attracted to Parker's body.

The kiss turned ravenous. Dallas cupped the back of Parker's head, refusing to allow him to break off the embrace.

Not that Parker had any plans of doing that. It felt like Dallas was trying to suck Parker's cock off by way of his tongue.

Drawing Parker's tongue into his mouth, Dallas sucked and stroked to the same rhythm he worked their cocks with, one large firm hand wrapped around Parker's dick while his own ground against Parker's flat belly.

Water splashed and trickled between them, teasing Parker's skin, a sharp contrast to the firm tugs, tight massaging grip and hungry, heated kisses. His ass was flattened against the cold tile but his head was held in a protective grip off the hard surface. The steaming shower spray felt tepid compared to the building heat coursing though his body. Parker was lightheaded, his climax coiling behind his balls, his cock stiff and swollen. His mind linked the sensation of the warm lips ravishing his mouth directly to his groin, the bobbing sucking sensation reaching down to encompass his shaft, every swipe of Dallas's wet, rough tongue interpreted as a pre-cum slicked tug on his cock.

Suddenly Dallas groaned into the kiss, the sound low, primal and satisfied. New warmth smeared into Parker's belly, the drawn out groan vibrating through their chests. The realization their kiss had been enough to send Dallas off triggered Parker's orgasm. He shuddered, fingers digging into muscle, back arched to shove his hips and dick hard into Dallas's flesh. The hand around his cock disappeared, only to reappear a second later cupping his ass and pulling him painfully closer.

Even after the glow of climax faded the kiss continued, slowly gentling until it was barely a light touch. The pressure on his head slackened as Dallas kissed his way over Parker's face to nuzzle at the soft skin behind his ear.

His blood pressure roared in his head but Parker still heard Dallas utter what sounded like a fervent oath.

"Christ, you're a keeper, doc."

He didn't get a chance to comment. Still holding onto Parker's head and ass, Dallas swung them around so that the shower hit them full force, stripping away the sweat and cum. Parker stuck his head under the spray, shivering a little when Dallas turned down the temperature. The cool water brought a refreshing burst of energy back to his lethargic mind and limbs. He pulled away from Dallas's now unneeded grip, nodded without looking at his partner and hurriedly left the shower stall.

The sound of the shower being turned off and muffled footsteps followed him to the lockers. He picked up a towel off the bench and dried off in record time, wrapping it around his waist before turning around to face his companion. He hoped the sudden flush making his face warm would be attributed to the heat of the water or their recent exertions, but one look at Dallas's concerned expression and that hope died.

"Hey, you don't have to run away or be embarrassed about this. Come on, doc."

The man stood three feet away, a puzzled, sympathetic frown marring his rugged face. Dallas skipped any pretence at drying off, merely securing a towel low on his hips with a casual wrap and tuck. The still healing, shiny pink scar on the man's solid hip and thigh showed between the open edges. Parker found himself hoping the whole thing would give in to gravity and fall away, allowing him one last, full view of the man.

Dallas took a step toward him and Parker held out a restraining hand. "Who are you? Where do you work here?"

"Don't freak out on me, professor. You've got nothing to worry about. Nothing to be embarrassed about."

"Who *are* you? You look like a bodyguard."

"What? No. Christ." Dallas planted his hands on his hips, a reluctant twist to his mouth. After studying Parker for several tense seconds, he shook his head once, wasted a little more time rubbing a hand over his face, then nodded. "Fine. I'd rather have done this over breakfast or my place or your place, but... fine. You're obviously feeling used and embarrassed about this for some reason." He raised one defiant finger in the air and pointed it at Parker, lips pulled tight in a straight line. "You have no right to feel that way, either. This wasn't a drive by."

"Drive by? I don't know what that means. And I'm not embarrassed."

"Drive by. One night stand. Don't you *ever* go out socially?" Dallas straightened his shoulders as if he was adjusting a suit coat, a gesture Parker found puzzling considering the man was wearing only a towel. "Listen, doc. I don't do drama and I don't do meaningless casual. I'm an ex-Army Ranger. I'm a serious guy. And yes, you are embarrassed. Your face is so red you look sunburnt."

"That doesn't tell me who you are or your function in the company. And I'm *not* embarrassed."

"I don't work here."

Parker stepped back a pace. A flash of trepidation washed over him, but then he remembered the cardkey with Dallas's picture on it he had seen the one evening when they had arrived at the gym entrance at the same. Parker hadn't been able to read the name on it but the picture was definitely this man. Dallas had open the keyed, locked door for him so someone had cleared him through the company's rigorous security screening and allowed him access to the building.

"Don't get all freaked out on me, doc." Dallas leaned against the lockers, his stance as casual and unthreatening as a life-sized statue of Hercules could be in a confined space. "I'm an agent with the FBI. Just transferred to the DC Bureau from New York. *Yes*, you are."

Ex-Army Ranger. Current FBI agent. No wonder the guy was built like a freight train. That was unexpected. Cool, but still unexpected. "What's the FBI doing *here*, Agent Dallas?"

"Agent Wade. Dallas is my first name."

"Agent Wade. Wade?" Parker blinked and self-consciously stood a little taller. He had to make a grab for his towel when the slight movement sent it slithering off his narrow hips. "Like in *Austin Wade*? The company's CEO?"

"Yeah. Just like that. My parents are from Texas." A wicked smirk smoothed away the pursed frown and defensive glare. "Austin's my older brother."

He motioned vaguely at the scar on his hip and thigh. "I'm on medical leave, recuperating from a... work related injury.

Austin suggested I work out here for a couple of weeks while I get settled into the area, instead of joining a gym. It works for me." He grabbed another clean towel and mopped off his face, running it over his short dark hair, leaving it standing tall in a rakish, spiky look. Looking back up, he caught Parker's still stunned gaze. "Worked out in a couple of good ways, if you know what I mean."

Parker could feel his eyes pop open wide. "I just...." He pointed in the direction of the sauna and then the shower. "With my *boss's* brother? A *Federal* agent? On *company* property?" His voice rose an octave with each question but the last came out a whisper. "Holy *crap!*"

A genuinely amused smile beamed across Dallas's face, a gleam of shared secrets in his eyes. "I won't tell, if you won't tell."

Still wide eyed, Parker fidgeted but managed to hold Dallas's gaze. This was the best thing that had happened to him in years. Maybe his lifetime. This guy was a freaking walking, talking statue of David. Plus he was funny, sincere, and oddly tender during sex for the he-man type. It didn't hurt any that his smile made firecrackers explode in Parker's stomach and his cock act like it had a permanent penile implant jacking it up.

Parker took a hesitant step forward, lessening the distance between them. "I'm not worried about telling."

"Yeah?"

"Yeah... ah, no." Parker shook his head, too distracted to work out the tough guy shorthand Dallas used to communicate with. "I mean *yeah*. I *mean*, I'm not worried about that."

"No?" Dallas's expression turned cautious as Parker took another step toward him, but the gleam in his eyes said 'bring it on' when Parker let the hastily gathered edges of the falling towel slip from his fingers. "What are you worried about then?"

"Not worried. And not embarrassed." He stepped into Dallas's personal space, immediately reaching up with one hand to tug the man's grinning face down to his level. He pulled at the tucked hem of Dallas's towel until is fell to the floor at their feet.

"Just… formulating a hypothesis on how best to execute my approach. You're twice my size. It presents… logistical problems." He tugged on Dallas's shoulders until the man lowered his lips to graze over Parker's talking mouth. "Unless of course, you'd prefer to continue in the role of dominant aggressor and," he swallowed hard, his breathing growing shallow and rapid, his tongue darting out to hesitantly lick at Dallas's waiting, silent mouth, "and use your considerable strength to hold me, equalizing the differences between—"

"You were a lot quieter when you were confused." A blistering kiss prevented any response. When the embrace finally broke, slightly breathless, Dallas added, "But this is pretty cute, too."

"I'm *not*—" Parker hoped the flush burning his cheeks would be mistaken for embarrassment instead of the burst of excitement that rushed through him.

"Yeah. You are. Small, sexy and smarter than *shit*. And clueless and confused and damn *cute*. Learn to live with it, doc." Dallas stroked his thumb down the arch of Parker's neck, chin to sternum, a slow, tender, appreciative touch. "I plan on learning to."

THE DRIVE HOME

LAURA BAUMBACH

The shower was a huge walk-in, built into one entire end of the spacious room. It sported a deep trough, several drains, and four-foot walls on either side of the opening. The walls had double showerheads on adjustable arms at various heights all around the large, tiled cubicle.

There were little cubby nooks at staggered heights embedded in the walls, each equipped with a thick metal rod handgrip. Two of the higher rods had an old-fashioned soap on a rope laced around each of them.

Rick pressed Adam up against the cold tile wall between the soaps. Adam gasped and his cock wilted a little at the shock. Gooseflesh broke out over his flesh and he shivered. His hands clenched hard on Rick's shoulders, leaving finger shaped marks in the heated skin.

Rick moaned and dropped his head into the crook of Adam's neck, burying his face and inhaling. "God, the way you smell." He licked his way up Adam's neck and jaw, pulling his lover's face down by a firm grip in his hair. He murmured over the man's mouth, sucking gently on one swollen lip then the other. He ran his hands up and down Adam's thighs wrapped around his waist then slid his hands under his firm ass, where he roughly fondled the tight globes, brushing lightly over Adam's opening.

Adam shuddered and sighed at the teasing touch from the hot, thick fingertips.

"Oh, yeah." Rick held Adam in place with the sheer power and weight of his body while he raised one of Adam's arms over their heads. Grabbing one end of the soap rope, he pulled until the soap slid up to the grab bar then looped the rope securely around Adam's wrist twice. Staring Adam in the eye, he did the same to the other wrist with the second soap rope.

Adam stared back, obviously startled, but willing to play along. He wasn't going to stop now. Even if he wanted to, his cock wasn't going to let him. It stood straighter, taller and more eager with each turn of the ropes. By the time Rick was done restraining him, Adam was panting and straining against the light bonds. He rested his head back against the cool tiles and looked up at Rick, thrilled by the hard, possessive look on Rick's chiseled face. He and Rick had only been hooking up for little over a month. Each time they met was a new adventure. Rick liked to experiment and so long as it felt good, Adam was willing to play along. So far, everything had felt *very* good.

Taking a savage, deep throated kiss from Adam, Rick slowly released his hold. He let Adam's legs slide to the floor. He stepped back, his gaze lingered over Adam's body, taking extra time at Adam's swollen, parted lips, the deep purple mark on his arched neck a testament to the last time they had fucked. His stare dropped to the thin trail of dark hair that led to Adam's flat stomach and slightly curved, beckoning cock.

Rick licked his lips. He turned on the water, adjusted the temperature and began directing showerheads to spray over Adam.

"Going to make you so hot. Slick." Rick moved forward again and tugged on the ropes. He licked playfully over Adam's lips, but kept their bodies from touching. "I want to hear you scream my name."

Adam's voice was husky with need. "I can do that now. Just touch me." His dark eyes pleaded, the pupils dilated with desire. He whispered back into Rick's still hovering mouth. "Please."

Still keeping his physical distance, Rick's lips brushed over Adam's mouth with each word he spoke. "Bet on it, babe."

Warm water pulsed onto Adam's chest and sides. A second showerhead sprayed a teasing, fine mist over his groin. He spread his legs to let the trickling water run in rivulets over his aching balls.

Air thick and heavy, clouds of moisture filled the room with a ghostly haze. A fine sheen of sweat popped out on his face. Adam squirmed against the cool tiles at his back. A slight tug on his arms reminded him of his helpless position and made his cock harden as it grew heavier with each pull on the ropes.

Rick selected a soft, scratchy net ball and a bottle of tinted gel. Standing directly in front of Adam, he soaped up the sponge and worked the ball into a foamy lather, his intense stare riveted on Adam's face.

Starting at Adam's up-stretched arms, Rick worked the sponge down the front of Adam's body, stroking and caressing every square inch of skin above the other man's waist. He concentrated on sensitive armpits and Adam's chest, lavishing the lean muscles and straining tendons with multiple layers of silky foam. Adam's nipples received extra attention, the sponge pressed more firmly against the erect nubs, swiping again and again with the silky rough surface of the netting until Adam was moaning.

"Tell me what you need." Rick encouraged in a sultry whisper.

Adam moaned, closed his eyes and shook his head.

"Tell me." Rick lightened his strokes until Adam was arching off the wall to maintain contact. "Tell me."

All contact disappeared. Adam's eyes popped open. He strained against his bonds and whimpered. "More." He was rewarded with the return of the silky caress. "Yeah, yeah. Ugh! Harder." Voice hoarse with need, Adam arched into the caress.

Rick slowly dropped to his knees. He trailed the sponge down one of Adam's sides then the other, following the curve of thigh down to the arch of each instep. He pointedly avoided Adam's bobbing erection, narrowly skimming down the crease of his groin and back up. The swollen shaft swayed, briefly leaking a milky fluid that was washed away in the warm mist of the shower's spray.

Adam looked down to see Rick's broad shoulders and short, water-darkened hair. Small streams ran down the tanned flesh as they followed the dips and valleys of well defined muscles and sinewy limbs.

He could see Rick's nipples were peaked and rosy, the flesh was full and erect like his own. Adam wanted to be able to lick and suck them. He moaned then whimpered, arms straining against his bonds. The impact of his loss of freedom growing even more torturous as desire and lust took control of him.

His desperate groan brought Rick up from his knees.

Sighing in relief, Adam nearly cried out when one of his wrists was released, fingers automatically reaching for Rick's smooth, water-slick chest. His relief was short lived.

"Fuck! Rick! What?" The last was more of a desperate whine than a question.

"Not yet." Rick bit the lobe of Adam's ear. The sharp tingle of pain made Adam shiver again. God, he was getting to like this too much!

Adam was spun around face to the wall then his wrist was tied next to his other bound wrist.

Rick nudged Adam's legs apart with his knee. He ran the slippery sponge down Adam's spine, letting the satiny smooth suds gather at the small of his back where they ran into the crack of his clenched ass. Rick followed the sudsy track with the net ball. He rubbed the gritty surface of the sponge over Adam's raw, fluttering asshole.

"So tight, so slick. Just right for the drive home." Rick scoured over the opening, adding just enough pressure to make the contact erotic, not teasing. "So slippery when wet."

Adam shoved his ass higher in the air and gasped. "Oh, god, yeah, more please."

Rick played with increasing pressure, varying the length and area he stroked, never giving Adam enough to reach a peak of excitement, but not allowing him to fall complacent either. He sponged lower over sensitive inner thighs, then forward to nudge the tight sac hanging unprotected and inviting between Adam's spread, trembling legs.

Adam wrapped his fingers around the cords binding his hands until his knuckles turned white, concentrating on every sensation his skin was transmitting to his fevered brain. He blocked out the sounds of the water and the soft murmur of Rick's breathing, trying to intensify the little thrills of excitement traveling up his spine from his ass. His cock thumped against the tile wall and he squirmed to feel the ridges of the grout where it met smooth tile.

Just as he found a rhythm and pace that fed his approaching climax, he was suddenly spun around and knocked against the wall. Looking up into Rick's face, Adam's breathing hitched.

"Uh-uh. No cheating." Rick held the sponge directly above Adam's erection. He squeezed a dollop of suds onto the reddened tip, letting the silky foam drizzle down the length of the heated rod.

Adam hissed and clenched his eyes, torn between shaking off the maddening tickle and savoring every slow oozing bubble on his sensitive skin. The sensation faded away as the fine spray of water pelted him. Adam realized that was all he felt. Opening his eyes he was greeted by a sight that took his already labored breath away.

Standing in front of him Rick basked under the shower spray, tall, broad shouldered, sharply defined in the bright light of the shower spotlights. Just out of reach.

Adam slowly raked his gaze up Rick's body, stopping at Rick's handsome, chiseled face. Rick's expression of primal hunger mirrored his own thwarted cravings. Adam squirmed at the thought of the imposing, restrained physical power of Rick's sexual side waiting to be unleashed.

"Like what you see?" Rick's voice was like a cat's purr, rumbled and silky rough. "Maybe you need to see more before you can decide?"

Rick flexed and stretched under the now pulsing spray of water, never lowering his lust filled gaze from Adam's face.

Adam's attention darted from one impressive muscle group to the next. Droplets of water, like tiny prisms refracted in the shower spotlights, rained down on the smooth, sun-darkened skin, highlighting every curve, bulge and smooth plane. Adam wanted to follow their glistening trail with his tongue, taste the amber flesh, smell the clean scent of skin. He moaned and strained against the ropes.

He watched as Rick deliberately struck a provocative pose. Rick jutted his tapered hips forward, forcing his fully engorged cock higher, letting the natural pulsing movement of the straining shaft mesmerize and taunt Adam.

Adding more gel to the sponge, Rick soaped and caressed his own body, swiping deliberately over the glistening flesh, purposely avoiding his groin. After the front of his body had been bathed, he dropped the sponge. Leisurely gelling his hand, he then brought it to his erection. Stroking the proud shaft in one meaty hand, he palmed and kneaded his chest with the other, working his nipples taut.

Adam felt his temperature rise and his breathing grow more labored with each pass Rick made over his shaft. He watched the man's thick, square shaped hand glide up and down, circling the bulbous head with his thumb and fingering the weighty sac nestled between his firm, stout thighs. Rick moaned, bringing Adam's attention back to his face.

"God, I'd love to feel your sweet lips wrapped around my cock, Adam. Love to have your hot, little tongue lapping at me," Rick stroked himself in time to the rhythm of his words, "licking out my slit," circling the head with his fingers, massaging the leaking fluid from the tip into his skin, "sucking my juice out of me."

Stepping closer, Rick pinched his nipples and rolled the peaks hard between his fingers. "All for you, Adam. It's all yours. Would you like that?" He dropped his gaze to Adam's straining cock and licked his lips provocatively, whispering in a throaty purr thick with desire. "Or would you like me to take your sweet, juicy rod down my throat? Swallow you whole? Suck the cum right out of you until your balls ache?"

Panting, Adam arched off the wall, trying to narrow down the distance separating them. The spray from the showerheads had turned from soothing to torturous, each new burst of water was like being pelted with sharp pins, and the comforting warmth of the water was now a stifling heat. He could feel his pulse pounding in the base of his cock, the shaft so hard and aching he thought the skin might split.

"Suck me!" Adam gasped. "Please, Rick, suck me. Fucker! Suck me dry."

Instantly closing the gap between them, Rick grabbed Adam's face, adding a light kiss to each eyelid before sealing his mouth to Adam's lips. Rick kissed him, deep and hard, pressing his heated body along Adam's slender frame.

Adam returned the kiss with fevered enthusiasm, biting and licking over Rick's lips, cheeks and jaw. As Rick drew away, Adam surged forward and sucked on the man's strong chin, mimicking the act he was requesting.

Running his hands down Adam's writhing body, Rick fell to his knees, nudging Adam's legs farther apart as he dropped. Without preamble or warning he took the slender, hard shaft into his mouth and began to slowly swallow it, inch by inch to draw out the moment.

Adam bucked, pumping his hips into the blissful heat of Rick's talented mouth, pulling the rope confining his wrists to its limit. A gel-slicked finger brushed over his hole then wormed its way into his ass, massaging and coating the tender insides. It was the added push Adam needed. Spurting and bucking into the tight suction of Rick's throat, Adam came. "Rick! Jesus, fuck!"

Adam felt like his balls were being sucked up through his cock. He was dizzy and disoriented from the heat and the rocketing swiftness of his orgasm. The moment he started to soften he was released, a hot hand replacing the hot mouth, skillfully fondling his half-hard cock to respond again.

Opening his eyes, Adam found himself facing the shower wall once more. Rick plastered his body to Adam's back and his throaty gravel voice, strained with pent up lust, panted in his ear. "God, you're so beautiful when you come. Stretched out and helpless, all hard and ready for me, begging for me."

Rough hands kneaded Adam's nipples. Rick moved his hand down to massage over Adam's backside, roughly spreading and gripping the firm globes, letting a rivulet of hot water run over the slicked, puckered opening.

Rick stroked Adam's erection back to fullness. "Want my cock buried deep inside of your tight little ass? Would that make you happy?" He jacked harder, his gel-slicked hand moving smoothly over the thickening rod, fingers rimming the tip and tracing the pattern of pulsing veins.

Adam grunted and pushed into the harsh grip, seeking more friction. "Fuck me. Just fucking fuck me."

Rick kissed his lover's shoulder then bit the curve of his neck, adding teeth marks to the purple bruise already branding Adam. With one powerful surge of lustful energy, Rick breached Adam's opening and plowed in to the hilt, driving the smaller man off the floor and up the wall. Rick held Adam in place with an arm around his waist and one under a bent leg, gripping the thigh hard enough to leave bruises.

Resting his forehead on the wall beside Adam, Rick whispered in his lover's ear while he pounded mercilessly into Adam's ass. "Feels so sweet, so tight. So good."

Adam reached up and grabbed hold of the metal bar the rope was tied to above his head. Pulling his body up, he shoved back against the iron rod sliding in and out of his opening, squeezing and twisting his ass with each brutal impact.

"Harder! Fuck me harder! Give it to me." Adam shuddered and trembled, impaled again and again on the thick, long rod so deep his stomach muscles fluttered. "Christ! Rick!"

The ripples of pleasure ran down Adam's rigid body, clenched around the cock still pounding into him. Rick gripped both of Adam's hips hard, heaving and pounding with a raw, primal energy, as if he was feeding off every quivering tremor. "Jesus God!"

A burst of pain mixed with a lightning quick blast of bright pleasure streaked up Adam's spine as Rick shifted slightly and hammered over his prostate. Adam tightened his muscles to recapture the sensation, feeling the shaft inside of him grow and pulse.

"So close. Almost there." Rick grunted and strained, his voice tight. "Gonna fill you up. No one can do you better." He arched his back and shoved deeper, gasping his words in hoarse, strangled breaths. "All. Fucking. Mine."

Adam felt the blast of cum flood his ass, amazed at the heat and volume of the load. Impaled motionless on Rick's spurting rod, he gasped and bucked as a new sizzle of excitement burned along his nerve endings. His over-sensitized body responded to the throbbing iron rod still bathing his inner walls with liquid heat, clenching. The broad cock head pulsed against his prostate and stretched his fluttering inner muscles to their limits. One last rapid, unexpected, brutal plunge in and out of his abused hole and Adam's cock spasmed and spurted, leaving a small smear of pale juice on the wall.

Dizzy from the heat and weak from the exertions, Adam looked over his shoulder. He croaked out the first words that came into his head. "You can drive me home any day."

THE

CATARACTS

PART ONE

WILLIAM MALTESE

CHAPTER ONE

This isn't the first time I've run.

At age fourteen, when my mother died of cancer, I ran. Oh, I didn't get far. I didn't have the money at my disposal, then, like now, to hop a plane to South America. Instead, I filled a paper bag with food from the kitchen and fled into the woods behind the house. My father found me, of course.

"Running never solves anything," he said.

He was always able to cope. Coping is something with which I sometimes have a problem. Maybe it was because my father or those people he hired – my father seldom around – were so good at coping for me.

Well, suddenly my father is dead, and there's no one to help me adequately cope with that.

Oh, Harold tries, but my being courted by an older man who is also the head of the modeling agency with which I'm signed, isn't what I'm looking for. Even if I have, for years, been contemplating sex with "some" man — thinking there has to be more than what I experience with my dick ejaculating up seemingly always available pussy; being assured by more than one of my fellow models, gay, in the fashion business that that *is* the case. Harold certainly isn't all that bad to look at and has never made any bones (although he has made plenty boners) about his wanting to be my first.

I am, in a way, then, suddenly running from Harold, too. He seemed genuinely hurt when I told him I was going off alone and didn't want him along for the ride.

"I'm a big boy," I said, feeling anything but my twenty-one years. "I can certainly take care of myself for a couple of weeks. Besides, it isn't as if it's all pleasure."

"But South America?" Harold moaned. "Couldn't you go somewhere a bit closer?"

"The property is in South America." I was more than a little piqued that I had to go through that redundant reminder. "I don't want to go *just anywhere* and mope."

I doubt that he really understands. I'm not sure I even understand — completely. My lawyer tells me the sale of the property can easily be taken care of without me going anywhere near it. International deals like this one are carried out every day of every year. Likely, I just hope the change of scenery will pull me out of my funk.

In the plane seat next to me, Cary Blight, whom I've met on the flight, stirs in his sleep, readjusting his position without coming awake.

I take a few minutes to scrutinize him closer. It isn't the first time I've done so. I spent the whole first hour of our flight admiring his masculine good looks while spilling my guts as regards my in-process runaway. In the end, I was embarrassed by my diarrhea of the mouth, and I'd apologized.

"Oh, don't be silly," he said, his rugged features breaking into an attractive smile that immediately turned the man into a boy. *Why isn't he the one trying to get into my pants?* "Any psychiatrist will tell you that unloading on a complete stranger is some of the best therapy around."

"Good for *me*, granted." I laughed. My right hand smoothed my light blonde hair out of my large gray eyes.

"Oh, I'm having a marvelous time," he said, all gentleman. "Actually, you could probably talk about anything and keep me interested."

I'm used to veiled and unveiled compliments, by men and women, by gays and straights. Once, I'd been insulted whenever someone only paid attention to my physical veneer and had no interest in what was beneath it. In time, however, I've come to accept that I'm attractive and that in a world where youth and beauty are admired, it's only natural that the first thing someone notices about me is how good I look. I was pleased that, up until then, though, Cary hadn't treated me as just another dumb, good-looking blond. He'd rambled off the technical aspects of his job as if I understood every word. I understood very little except that it has something to do with mining.

Cary moves again in his sleep, and lest he wake to discover me playing voyeur, I turn my attention back to the window.

Below is the jungle of Brazil: a deep green carpet that stretches for as far as the eye can see, interspersed with myriad ropes of waterways that curl, meander, and fold in on themselves until navigation of, and on, seems quite impossible.

It's hard to imagine that the civilized city of Rio is only hours behind me. Lovely, lovely Rio. I had lingered there for over a week, losing myself in its exotic spell. I was enthralled by its towering huge crags up-thrust within its city limits. I was caught up in the turnabout of seasons that put me in tropical heat while it's winter in London. The week of lying in my skimpy Brazilian swimming suit on the sands of Ipanema Beach toasted my pale skin a delightful shade of honey.

I would have stayed longer in Rio - I'd had actually been almost out of my depression, but Harold started calling nightly. Disturbed that he can't seem to leave me alone for just a couple of weeks, I've run even further.

Cary stirs again, stretches, and comes awake. I turn in his direction and smile. Sleepily, he smiles back and then checks his watch. He comes to a more substantial sitting position. He looks momentarily past me and to the window. He points.

"Thar she blows!" he says.

I turn back to the verdant river-veined jungle below.

There are volcanoes up and down the west coast of South America, but there aren't any of them here to account for the sudden visible steam on the horizon.

"Foz do Iquacu," he confirms in his slightly accented Portuguese.

I've picked up just enough of the language, in Rio, to know what he says. Frankly, though, I've not expected the spray to be visible from such a distance. "It must be huge," I decide aloud.

"There are actually hundreds of waterfalls and cascades," he says, "all plunging over the one escarpment. "One helluva sight, even from the air, as I think you'll agree. Unfortunately, that's the closest I ever seem to get, despite all of my intentions to the contrary. All a question of bad timing, I guess."

The pilot announces our descent. Cary and I check our seat belts and then go back to watching the cloud of spray growing upon our approach.

I see no signs of civilization until the plane banks right, then the runway and a small grouping of buildings come into view.

The plane lands, bounces twice before settling down to a fairly smooth glide to a stop.

"Well, good luck to you, then, William," Cary says, standing so that I can squeeze by him and enter the aisle first. I find our brief mutual rub-by arousing in the extreme. "Maybe we'll meet again."

"I'll be here for a while," I say. "If you're back through in the next week or so, give me a call. I'm staying at a local residence called *The Cataracts*."

"Are you now?" he sounds impressed. "Maybe I'll take you up on your invite." He smiles. "It's about time I see the falls from closer than five-thousand feet. I hear the view from where you'll be staying is genuinely spectacular."

"By the time you're back in the area, I'll perhaps have enough bearings to give you a personally guided tour," I hopefully, further entice.

Up the aisle, a stewardess goes through the final procedure for opening the door. I give one final nod to Cary and walk forward to be greeted by the hot blast of incoming air that suddenly engulfs me.

"English?" the man at customs asks, a minute or so later, taking my passport.

"*Si, pero hablo espanol,*" I reply, letting him know that I speak passable Spanish if he's more comfortable with that. One of the minor advantages to being in Iguassu is that I've crossed into Spanish-speaking Argentina and can now, once again, manage a halfway intelligent conversation.

"Mr. Maltese?"

I turn toward the voice and see the attractive young man standing about three feet away.

"I'm Jeremy Salinas," he says after I acknowledge my identity with a nod.

I expected someone far older. He's probably only two or three years my senior, if that.

"I've the car waiting," he says. "I've been looking forward to your arrival."

Clearing the terminal, after Jeremy's arrival, is a breeze. He seems to know everyone. I'm processed without anyone even bothering to look into my luggage. Jeremy carries my bags out to a Jeep parked out front.

"Did you have a good flight?" He ushers me into the passenger seat and closes the door behind me. He walks around the car and climbs behind the steering wheel.

"Quite enjoyable, thanks." Having left the air-conditioned terminal, I'm again aware of the high humidity and heat.

"I thought possibly you'd stay in Rio a bit longer," he says. He steers the car into sparse traffic.

"I was tempted," I admit. It's hardly prudent to mention the calls from Harold that see me in Iguassu sooner than either Jeremy or I expected.

"Ah, but I do love Rio," Jeremy says, steering into a left turn and heading us along a two-way paved road bordered by lush undergrowth. Just by the way he says what he says gives me the impression that he would rather be there than here at the moment.

"Gorgeous city," I admit.

"But, business in Iguassu before pleasure in Rio, yes, Mr. Maltese? May I call you William?"

"Please do." Since we're only separated by a few years - months? weeks? days?, it would sound ludicrous for either of us to preface every name-calling with *Mr.*

"You'll call me Jeremy, of course."

I turn my head slightly to get a better look at Jeremy's profile.

He's handsome. What, I now try to determine, makes him that way. As someone who has been acutely aware of attractiveness-versus-ugliness from my first modeling assignment at age four, I'm always interested in trying to determine just what combination of physical characteristics makes one person favorably stand out from all others.

To begin with, despite his name, Jeremy *Salinas*, doesn't look Spanish. He looks Italian. He has the classical features found on first-rate sculptures in the Vatican Museum. His hair is black and curly, and it's long enough to bang his forehead without looking scraggly. His eyelashes are long and exceptionally lush. A passing shaft of light gives evidence that his eyes are just as black as his hair. His nose is set nicely above kissable full lips.

He must feel my scrutiny, because he turns to me and smiles. He has white teeth. His left cheek dimples.

"I have high hopes that we'll be able to get our business quickly out of the way and get down to some fun and games before you have to leave," he says. "The place has been a bit too dreary for ever so long, and a nice party might be just what the doctor ordered."

"Whoever would we invite?" I'm glancing off to all sides of the road. We seem to be the only people within miles.

"You do have a point, there," he says and laughs. For some reason, I find his mirth just a shade off-key. Or, am I just imagining it? "However, there are a few people hidden out there who can be civilized if given a chance — in from the wild every ten years or so."

"Actually, I don't know why the lack of buildings surprises me," I say. "Rio certainly isn't indicative of all South America, is it?"

"Unfortunately, no." Again, there's wistfulness in his voice.

"Is it far, where we're going?" I'm bothered by a faint hum in my ears which I attribute to return to a lower altitude.

"Not horribly far, "he says. "I imagine you're ready for a nice hot shower and a fresh change of clothes."

"Is it always this warm and sticky?" What breeze there is isn't cooling.

"Pretty much, yes," he says, concentrating on the road ahead. "It'll be cooler at the house, though."

We ride in silence for a few minutes. The roaring in my ears gets louder. I pinch my nostrils with my right thumb and index finger and blow out my cheeks.

"Ears plugged?" He has witnessed my maneuver.

"I've suddenly a disconcerting inner-ear problem," I explain. "Humming."

He laughs. I detect a genuine amusement before lacking.

"It's just the river cataracts," he says. "You could blow until your brains came out both ears, and the sound wouldn't go away. Believe it or not, you'll get used to it."

I doubt that. The humming increases as the Jeep barrels down the virtually deserted roadway.

After another twenty minutes, the Jeep turns onto a dirt road and comes to a stop in front of a huge wrought-iron gate. Jeremy reaches across the seat toward the glove compartment. Does anyone actually wear gloves while driving, anymore, except race-car drivers?. His arm brushes my leg. I wonder if the contact is intentional. It lingers only for as long as it takes Jeremy to retrieve a small control box and push a button on it. The gate squeaks open.

Jeremy coaxes the Jeep through the opening. He pushes another button on the box, once the vehicle is through the breach. With a sound of metal grating against metal, the gate closes securely behind us.

Jeremy leans to replace the small black box but avoids any physical contact this time around.

"Is your brother going to be at the house?" I ask.

"My brother?"

"Kyle Salinas *is* your brother, isn't he?"

"Actually, he's my *half*-brother," Jeremy says. There's a slight tic in his left cheek. "Why would he be at the house, though?"

"He lives there, doesn't he?" I have the impression that Jeremy wishes I'd never brought up the subject of his half-brother. Still, I'm curious about Kyle Salinas. It wasn't Jeremy, after all, who originally wrote me to see if I would be interested in selling my share of the de Veer farm. I'd written Kyle back that I would certainly not be averse to his making an offer - that was the last I'd heard from him. It was a letter from Jeremy which submitted the bid I'd accepted; I've always assumed, though, that Kyle is in on the transaction.

"Actually, he's not around at the moment," Jeremy says. "Have you two met?"

"We only had brief correspondence."

"Kyle was thinking for a while of buying you out, too, was he?"

"You mean, your brother ... your half-brother... isn't party to your buy-out?"

"My brother is hardly in a financial position to buy anything at the moment," Jeremy says.

I let the matter drop. What business is it of mine who's buying my share of farmland? From what I can see, there isn't much in the area but jungle, jungle, and more jungle, filled with God-only-knows how many unfriendly plants, insects, and wildlife.

It's half an hour before the jungle stops and the manicured lawn begins. At the other end of the lawn sits a truly magnificent architectural structure, one wing of which actually climbs the branches of a huge tree.

"Welcome to *The Cataracts*, William Maltese," Jeremy says, taking the circular drive that deposits us at the front door steps.

The roaring in my ears is louder.

A small man appears out of seeming nowhere to give me the once-over and give Jeremy a frown.

"Take Mr. Maltese's bags up to his room, Carlos, then put the car in the garage," Jeremy says.

"Si, senor Jeremy," the small man says. His grin reveals two missing front teeth.

"If you'll come with me, William?" Jeremy motions me toward the stairs leading up to the front porch. I follow.

The door opens before we reach it. A figure seems completely to fill the opening.

Jeremy stops dead-still. Also, he turns decidedly pale.

"Welcome home, little brother," the figure in the doorway says. "Have a nice trip?"

"Kyle," Jeremy says finally.

"Surprised?" Kyle Salinas asks, not having moved.

My eyes are riveted on Kyle. He's a big, powerful man, well over six-feet. He's tanned deep chestnut. His muscled body is ill-contained in tight-fitting shirt, form-fitting riding breeches, and English riding boots.

"Why should I be surprised?" Jeremy literally wrings his hands, and then wipes his palms on his trousers.

"Pedro!" Kyle's head turns back toward the inside of the house. He steps aside to let a heavy-set man waddle onto the front porch. "I want you to take Mr. Maltese up to his room and make him comfortable."

"Kyle, I ..." Jeremy begins but stops.

"The library, Jeremy, if you please!" Kyle says. Without even looking at me, he turns and disappears into the house. Jeremy follows, rather (I think) like a whipped puppy.

I stand where I am, having been frankly fascinated by the whole scenario.

"Senor Maltese, *por favor,"* Pedro says, indicating that I should please follow him. Carlos, with my bags, follows me.

CHAPTER TWO

The view from the balcony of my assigned room is fantastic. The whole back of the house hugs a huge drop-off. Below, among the rugged rocks, the Parana River rushes towards its eventual meet-up with the Atlantic Ocean at Buenos Aires. Off to my left, the river meanders through a lush maze of small islands before tumbling into the chasm. Across the gorge, one immense wall of water pours amid constantly dull roaring. Standing at the edge of the balcony, I feel the spray from the deluge. It's a welcome relief from the heat of the fading day.

I would like to stay outside longer to let the magnitude of the wild and watery panorama sink in, Pedro urges me inside, though, to the tamer hot water of the bath he's drawn in a large claw-legged tub.

Soon, left alone, soapy liquid sensuously sloshes around, over, and under my cock and balls; my dick appreciatively swells to an erection.

My intention is to grab hold and pump my boner to a quick and speedy orgasm. Whipping it to climax seems the easiest way to take care of it. It's to be a jack-off purely for the sake of jacking off; nothing more complicated than that. Except, after a few speedy strokes of my fist, up and back, along the shaft of my erection, I add the fantasy of Cary Blight sucking my dick.

The male-male implication of my make-believe isn't anything that causes me concern, at this time in my life. It once did, before I came to accept that I was either bisexual or even completely gay, but I've since passed beyond any oh-God-no stage. Having accepted the likelihood that I will one day, sooner or later, have sex with a man, I've come to figure that I might as well, in the interim, likewise expand my sexual fantasies to include them.

"Yeah, buddy, suck it!" I tell my fist that's masquerading as Cary's hot and hungry mouth.

I hook my legs up and over their respective sides of the tub, letting my wet feet drizzle water onto the tile of the bathroom floor. The maneuver elevates my ass, the crease of which is now slid by the soapy fingers of my free hand until I've located my water-soaked pucker. I play with my winked sphincter; even poke the tip of my fuck-finger into it, while my jack-off commences an even swifter beating rhythm up and down my stiff dick.

I don't know exactly when my fantasy lover metamorphoses from Cary Blight to Jeremy Salinas. Maybe it happens when I fuck my finger so far into my butt that it finds my prostate, punches it, and triggers the oozing of pre-cum from my cock's mouth to mingle with the soap slicking my pumping fist; that's when I say, "Yes, Jeremy, fuck my virgin asshole!" My fuck-finger stabs deeper. "Show this silly virgin ass what it's been missing!"

My hand whips. My hips take up an automatic swing from my hooked-over-the-edges-of-the-tub legs.

Wet sounds fill the room.

Bath water sloshes to overflowing.

I'm beating my meat way too fast and furious for my jack-off to last very long.

Already, my nuts are no longer suspended in a flaccid scrotum. The containing sac is taut around its contents. My testicles are aligned side-by-side. I know — by the sensations building inside of me — by having seen my balls' reactions to more than one impending orgasm and shoot-off — that soon my left nut will elevate slightly higher than my right, and a rip-roaring orgasm will soon ...

"Oh, yes, Jeremy!" My finger dives deeper up my ass and twists there. "Fuck ... suck ... shit ... damn ... whore ... yes ... yes ...

My dick shoots its load. The initial canon-shot splashes and drools my chin.

"Oh, *Kyle*, you sexy fucking stud!" I say with a loud grunt as a second wad of spunk shoots farther than the first — to smear my cheek.

Which leaves me a tad disconcerted. Sex with Kyle Salinas, in fantasy or reality, has never — ever — consciously crossed my mind. That I should suddenly put him in the line-up of potential candidates for my deflowering, my having so enjoyed his part-played in my just-finished fantasy that my nuts shot spunk particularly far and wide, leaves me curious — to say the least.

In the aftermath, latticed with my man-cream, more sense about me, I'm convinced that what happened is merely a weird anomaly played on me by my jet-lagged subconscious. I'm convinced that sex with the bully Kyle is not something I want now, or will ever want, even if — fat chance — it was ever offered.

Cleaning up the spermal stew I've made, using more soap and water, I try my best to remember what Kyle even looks like.

Black hair. I'm sure of that. Black *and* thick. Not wavy like Jeremy's but tousled. It hangs over Kyle's forehead, strand tips touching his long black lashes. It covers his ears.

His eyes are purple. I'm sure of that, too, because he's the first man I've ever seen with violet eyes.

His jaw is square. His chin is one of those deep clefts that always has me wondering how someone shaves inside it.

He has high cheekbones and, possibly, a dimple in his right cheek. The latter is purely speculation, since he definitely wasn't smiling when I saw him.

Kyle's shirt was open at his neck. Curly black hair in the breach? Yes. And, his arms were large, muscled, and tanned. His hands were large.

My imagination checks out his belly and even lower to the bulge that signifies ...

Suddenly, my dick is re-hardening.

"Finished?" Pedro inquires, in Spanish, through the closed door, and interrupts my reverie.

"Un momento!" The last thing I want is to arise from the bubbles — *Adonis from the Sea?* — with a boner for Pedro to see.

I reach for a towel and do my best to drape my stiffening prick. I make all attempts to will myself to softness but only achieve partial success before Pedro opens the door, uninvited, and comes in.

"I've unpacked your clothes," he says. "Do you need help getting dressed?"

"I'm fine, thank-you," I insist.

"Supper is promptly at eight," he says. "Mr. Salinas dresses for his evening meal."

Opposed to what? Coming to the meal naked?

"Mr. Salinas will be staying on, then?" I've no doubts that the Mr. Salinas to whom Pedro and I refer is Kyle and not Jeremy.

"Sí," Pedro says and waddles toward the door after giving me a look entirely inscrutable.

I dry more completely and stand in front of the full-length mirror that covers one bathroom wall. I let the boner-concealing damp towel sink to the floor and eye myself critically.

I spend a lot of time in the gym. I have a well-developed chest with square and naturally hairless pectorals. I have a naturally hairless washboard stomach with indented navel. I have a cock that is seven inches long when soft. When hard, like it is now, it's seven-and-a-half inches — neither too long, nor too short, nor too narrow, nor too thick-at least in my estimation.

I walk into the other room. It's large. The bed is four-poster. Rich wood paneling covers most of the walls, interspersed occasionally by swaths of dark Prussian-blue wallpaper. Heavy wooden beams are exposed as they support the high ceiling. The room has a decidedly masculine edge.

I walk to the door leading to the balcony and throw it wide. My ears are immediately assaulted by the sound of the gallons of water pouring unceasingly into the rocky cauldron below.

I stand naked until my flesh begins to goose-bump in the rising mist. Chilly as my body becomes, my dick hardens even more.

The sun has gone down, leaving a dim twilight.

I go back inside, shiver slightly, and pull the door closed behind me.

It's later than I think. I'll be lucky to get dressed before the eight o'clock deadline. What with the other excitement of the day, I doubt Kyle Salinas will be appreciative if I stroll in late.

At two minutes of eight, I open the door of my assigned quarters and step into the hallway. I find myself once again enveloped within chocolate woodwork. The upcoming balustrade is suspended halfway between the ceiling and the ground floor. Above me is a network of woodwork covered with intricately carved designs hardly seen from my level, let alone from the main floor farther below.

I look down into a room filled with its dark-leather furniture. The wood floor is covered with animal skins. There are elephant tusks crossed against one wall. I try to remember if there are elephants in South America. I don't think so.

"Ah, Mr. Maltese." Kyle is immediately below me, looking up. "I'm glad you're as punctual as you are handsome."

I descend the stairs.

"You're hardly what I expected," he says by way of additional greeting.

"What exactly were you expecting?" I'm curious.

"Let's just say you don't look all that conspiratorial."

"I beg your pardon?"

"You carry off feigned surprise very well, too," he says.

"I genuinely don't have a clue what you mean," I say.

"Sure you do," he disagrees.

Right then and there, I'm tempted to tell Kyle Salinas to take his meal and shove it up his sexy ass, but I'm hungry, not having eaten anything all day except for the continental breakfast at my hotel in Rio. I'm not counting that cardboard lunch on the airplane.

Kyle leads the way into a hallway and through a pair of open doors that entrance a large formal dining area.

"Even enemies should be able to enjoy a truce over a good meal," he says to me over one impressive shoulder.

"Enemies? Why are we enemies?" I'm confused.

"I'm talking about the deal you've apparently made with my half-brother," he says. For just an instant, I think I see a slight breach in his cool and calm façade. That breach, though, if there even is one, is short-lived.

"The deal I've made with Jeremy?" He's makes it sound less straight-forward than it is.

"Let's eat, shall we?" He stops at the table, pulls out one chair, and waits for me to do the same at the second place setting.

"Your half-brother isn't joining us, then?"

"My half-brother is a bit indisposed at the moment," he says cryptically.

A young man appears with a tureen of hot soup

"*Chupe a limena,*" Kyle says. "Prawns, fish, cheese, potatoes, lemon, and a few other sundry items."

When we've finished with the soup, having eaten it in silence, it's removed and replaced by a meat course.

"*Cuyes a la criolla,*" Kyle says and smiles at me over a forkful. "Guinea pig."

I refuse to let the image of some little pet, spinning in a wheel in its cage, before being taken out for baking, throw me. "Delicious." I take another bite.

"Mmmmmm, yes, rather," he confirms.

We revert to silence, and eventually dessert appears. It's some kind of custard with accompanying red berries.

When we're both finished, I say, "If you'll excuse me, I think I'll go to bed."

"I think not," he says. "Let's talk, now, since we managed so little of it throughout supper."

"I am very tired, Mr. Salinas."

"Do you call Jeremy, Mr. Salinas, too?" he asks.

I don't answer. He smiles. He does, indeed, have a dimple in his right cheek.

"I thought not," he says. "So, why don't you call me Kyle, and why don't I call you William?"

"What is it you want to talk about, *Mr. Salinas*?" I ask him.

"I want *The Cataracts*," he says.

I'm surprised. "You already *have The Cataracts*, don't you?"

"I have forty-five percent of it," he says. "Jeremy has forty percent; forty-five when you consider he controls Jenny's five. You have ten percent."

"*I* have ten percent *of The Cataracts*?" That's certainly news to me.

He eyes my surprise with a hint of genuine surprise of his own.

"Isn't that what this is all about?" he asks.

"I thought it was about the de Veer farm."

"This *is* the de Veer farm," he says, leans back in his chair, eyes me carefully. 'Farm' has been somewhat of a misnomer for quite some time. Initially, it was owned by my mother's first husband, Klan de Veer, with whom your father was acquainted when they were working a drilling operation together in Maracaibo."

I neither confirm nor deny. I didn't know any of what he's just said. I only know that there was the lone sheet of paper, amid so many others, among my father's many miscellaneous (and usually worthless) papers, dug out for closer inspection only after I received Kyle's initial letter of inquiry.

"Klan died," Kyle says, "and my mother married my father. He had money and had long coveted my mother and this particular patch of land. He's responsible for the present house and for me. Neither he nor my mother were aware they weren't complete owners of the estate until the loan papers concerning your father's share came to light from an old desk drawer."

I reach for the Baccarat crystal goblet that holds the last of my dessert wine. I sip the well-aired liquid, swallowing its delicious sweetness.

I want Kyle to go on. I wait. It's rather fascinating to think that my being here is due to some haphazard discovery of a loan paper in some old desk drawer. I doubt very much if I would have ever paid any attention to the record of the transaction at my end. Dad loaned so many people money in his lifetime, none of it repaid or backed by viable collateral, that ten percent of some South American dirt farm, even if I had discovered it earlier, wouldn't likely have seemed worth my effort to track down.

"Really, Mr. Maltese," Kyle says. "Is it really necessary for me to go over facts we both know you know?"

"I don't know anything about anything," I admit. "I didn't even know of my father's dealings with your father — or, if I did, I paid very little attention to having noticed them in passing — until you expressed interest in my share of the de Veer property."

"You'll excuse me if I find that a little hard to believe?"

"Feel free to believe whatever you please." I'm magnanimous. "Do you know how many uncollected and worthless IOUs my father had stuffed in all sorts of drawers, and nooks and crannies, when he died?"

"Why come all of this way when you could have sold your share, using lawyers?"

The answer to that, of course, is integrated with my personal problems which are really none of Kyle Salinas's business.

"One more thing," Kyle says. "If you were so convinced the property was of so little seeming value, why did you ignore my bid and wait for my brother's higher offer?"

"Maybe because you never got around to submitting an actual bid?" I suggest.

"Goddamn-it, the cunning little bastard!" Kyle says and stands so suddenly his chair almost tips without his making any effort to prevent it.

I get to my feet if just to eliminate the sudden sense of dominance he's achieved in towering over me.

"I presume you can find your way back to your room, Mr. Maltese." he says. It's not a question.

He turns, and leaves the room.

CHAPTER THREE

I awake to the night, knowing I'm not alone in my room. A chill goes up and down my spine before settling in the bottoms of my feet.

"William?" a voice hisses.

The voice isn't familiar - most voices distort when hissed.

"It's Jeremy."

I sit up. Sometime during the night, I've thrown off my blankets and am stark naked atop the sheet. I tug a section of blanket modestly over my crotch. Simultaneously, I stretch for the bedside lamp.

The light comes on.

"I have to talk to you," Jeremy says. Standing in front of the balcony door, he moves deeper into the room.

"Wouldn't this little chat wait until morning?"

"Do you think Kyle is letting me near you in the morning?" he asks with a little laugh. He plops sexily in a chair near the bed. He looks tired, though, and more than a little rumpled.

"Aren't you old enough to make such decisions for yourself?" I'm even more curious about this odd relationship with his half-brother.

"He had me locked in my room all evening," he says. "I had to shimmy the outside wall to reach your balcony."

"You what?" I try to remember anything to hold onto along the outside of the building.

"Held captive in my own home," Jeremy says. He doesn't sound as surprised as I think he should be.

"Surely, your brother … your half-brother … can't do that." I'm still trying to imagine Jeremy Salinas hanging like a human fly to some small ledge outside, nothing below him but rocks, boiling water, and empty air.

"He can do anything here that he damned well pleases," Jeremy says. "Stick around for a while, and you'll soon find that out."

"How can he possibly get away with that?"

"The servants fawn over him like bees over honey. They eat out of his hands."

"Surely, there are laws, even in this country." It sounds so Middle Ages to keep one's rival in the equivalent of a castle dungeon.

"Laws?" His laugh is short and dry. "Kyle is the law around here."

"How is that possible?" The very idea that Kyle Salinas can set himself up as some type of feudal lord, answerable to no one but himself, seems impossible in this day and age, even in South America.

"He's one of *them*," Jeremy says.

"One of whom?" Why is it that with Kyle and now Jeremy, I'm forever getting the impression I've come in mid-conversation?

"He was born here. He was raised here. He's always lived here. I'm the outsider."

"And that makes a difference?"

"Everyone see me as the interloper. It doesn't help that I'm trying to get rid of this place. That has Kyle, and a lot of the locals, very uptight."

"But he'd actually hold you here against your will?"

"Oh, he'd prefer me gone for good, but under his conditions," he says. "The happiest day of his life will be when I pull up and leave."

"So, why doesn't he just buy you out?"

"With what? He's as broke as I am, or did I fail to mention that?"

"You're broke?" His revelation — *slip of the tongue?*— is surprising.

"Oh, there's plenty of money to be made in selling," Jeremy says. "But, do you think Kyle will condescend to part with his share?"

"The amount of money you've offered for my percentage would hardly indicate you poor as the proverbial country church mouse."

"International Hotels has offered Kyle and me a substantial amount of money for our shares. They've agreed to advance me the money, against my share, to buy you out."

"A hotel chain?"

"Great place for a hotel, don't you think? Beautiful view. Cataracts and falls to rival Victoria or Niagara, and an airport that can be enlarged with little effort to take the bigger jets. It's a natural for the tourist trade. I could go anywhere on my share, live as I please, do what I want. But, Kyle won't cut his damned umbilical cord to this mausoleum." He slams the flat of his right hand against his thigh. "He's fucking out of his mind."

His face is flushed. He has little red splotches that stand out even through the tan of his dark-complexioned cheeks. His shirt is ripped in front (from his adventure on the outside wall?). A swath of hairless bronze flesh is seen through the cloth shreds.

"You will help me get out of here, won't you, William?"

"Is it so bad here?" I find the house quite pleasant. Actually, I find it downright palatial. I can see how Kyle might feel chagrined at his brother's attempts to sell it.

"Bad, you ask?" Jeremy asks incredulously. He goes to the balcony door and opens it. The roar immediately fills the room; I realize suddenly it's the same sound which had awakened me when Jeremy clandestinely entered the room. "Listen to that racket," he says. His voice is barely audible even though he's obviously talking loudly. He slams the door with such force that its glass rattles. "That noise can eat into your brain and drive you crazy."

He puts his hand to his forehead. I don't remind me that he's told me previously how one gets used to the sound. His skin looks hot.

"Jeremy, are you all right?"

He looks at me for a moment and, then, says, "I don't want to die like my mother, William. If I stay in this place, I know I won't any more survive it than she did."

He walks closer to the bed.

"This isn't me - this house, these falls, this wilderness," he says. "It's all an alien world. Everybody is right. I am an interloper here. I'll die if I have to stay here. Kyle doesn't care. If I walked out on that balcony this very minute and stepped over the edge, Kyle would merely exhale one very big sigh of relief."

"I rather doubt that, Jeremy. He is your half-brother, after all."

"There's an old Arab saying about brothers," he says. "Are you familiar with it?"

Frankly, I can't think of one.

"My cousins and I against the world," he says. "My brother and I against my cousins. I against my brother."

My eyes are again drawn to the rip in his shirt, possibly as a means of avoiding the pathetic pleading in his eyes.

"You will help me, won't you, William?" he asks. "Tell me that you haven't changed your mind?"

He looks desperate, frantic, and helpless. By contrast, he'd seemed so in control when he'd met me at the airport. He'd seemed so in control on the drive back to the house. All of that composure, however, suddenly evaporated the minute Kyle Salinas opened the front door.

"Do you have the papers you want me to sign?" I ask. It's rather pathetic the way his eyes light up like those of a drowning man to whom I've just thrown a lifejacket.

The shine in his eyes goes out. "Kyle searched my room and found them, but I'll get them back. You'll really sign them, yes?"

I'm not sure just what I'm feeling at the moment. I do know I'm confused by how my cock is hardening with attending fantasies as to how, were I so inclined, I could likely easily take advantage of Jeremy, and his studly body, in more ways than one.

The bedroom door suddenly flies open, banging the wall as it does so."Well, well," Kyle Salinas says, standing in the doorway just as he stood the doorway at the front of the house. "I thought maybe I'd find my wandering little brother here. Sure enough, here he is."

"And, *you're* here, just why?" I asked sarcastically.

"No need to ask why Jeremy is here," Kyle ignores my question. "Not by the size of the boners the both of you are sporting."

Blushing, I'm acutely aware of my stiffening dick apparently so obvious beneath its bit of blanket. Automatically, I single out Jeremy's crotch, and, sure enough ...

"Jeremy, go back to your room," Kyle says.

Without protest, Jeremy moves quickly past his half-brother and out into the hallway. Kyle closes the door and leans against it. He folds his arms across his chest and gives me a none-too-sincere smile.

"Not really quite the innocent you pretend, are you, William?"

"I haven't a clue what you're trying to get at. I only know that you've Jeremy so worked up that he was playing human fly out over the chasm outside."

"So, that's how he managed to join you undetected, is it?"

"He could have been killed."

Kyle shrugs as if that suggestion isn't as bad-news as I might intend.

"Just what new mischief were you and my half-brother contemplating, I wonder, other than hot sex?"

"I did come here to sell him something, didn't I?"

"Actually, it's not my half-brother to whom you'd actually be selling but to a hotel conglomerate. Did he bother to tell you that?"

"As a matter of fact, he did."

"Honor among thieves?"

"I beg your pardon?"

"Neither of you is stealing this place out from under me."

"Disposing of what's ours is hardly stealing, nor has it ever been."

"And if the process of disposing what is yours, you, also, dispose of what is mine?"

"In a democracy, the majority rules."

"That might very well be," he says. "But you'll soon discover this is no democracy you've stumbled into. Certainly, don't count on me going off on any more of Jeremy's cleverly maneuvered wild-goose chases so he can arrange for my Jeep to break down in the middle of nowhere while he meets up with you."

"That cryptic remark is supposed to have some meaning for me, is it?"

"It means that I'm not going to be so obliging as time marches on."

"Would you mind going away and coming back when you're better prepared to make more sense?"

He pushes away from the closed door on which he's been leaning and approaches me on the bed. Reflexively, I cover more of my nakedness, boner included, with the available bedding.

"Only interested in boys like my half-brother, William?" Kyle asks. "I would have thought you'd find a real man far more to your liking."

"Bring on a real man, and I just might. Until then, why don't you quit playing little bully-boy long enough for me to get some sleep? We can resume this conversation, with hopefully more sense to be made of it, in the morning."

"Jeremy offering you more than just money for your part in this little conspiracy?"

He stands over me. I'd get up to be on equal footing with him if I wasn't sure I might leave my covers behind. I'd feel very vulnerable completely naked *and* with a hard-on.

"Come on now, William. A handsome man of your experience certainly can't be long be amused by the likes of my half-brother. I might not have the money to offer that Jeremy 's backers can, but I can do far better in certain other departments."

He steps closer.

"There are some things better than money, William."

"Funny, but I'm not seeing that from where I am."

He steps back, does an about-face and leaves the room, slamming the door behind him.

CHAPTER FOUR

I stretch luxuriously, open my eyes, and realize, with a start, where I am.

I sit up and wonder how in the hell I slept so late. The answer, of course, is that what sleep I was getting last night was interrupted, and I hadn't gotten any more until nearly four o'clock this morning.

I throw back my blankets and crawl out of bed. I walk my usual morning woody to the door that I open onto the chasm outside. Clouds of mist are interspersed with shafts of sunlight within the abyss. It makes for a very pretty picture, especially as played out before the backdrop of lush greenery.

I look for the ledge along the outside of the house, to which Jeremy had clung precariously, last night, when he'd accessed my room. I find it and wouldn't have used it for love or money. Kyle can accuse his half-brother of many things but certainly not of physical cowardice.

The shower is separate from the tub. There are several nozzles, above and on all sides.

Water, when it hits my erect dick from certain angles, usually focused on that part of my cock-belly where corona attaches to shaft, is masturbatory. Such stimulation, often all of the way to orgasm, is better achieved in some showers than in others. Some showers don't have enough water pressure to provide orgasm. Or, the nozzles aren't attached at the right angles to do the job. No matter what way I turn in the multiple sprays of this shower, though, it's the right pressures at the right angles. I resign myself to the inevitability of orgasm during wash-up.

I can probably find some way to stand out of the way of the sensuous splatter. I can, at the very least, hurry up and turn off the water before it succeeds in doing what it's out to do. Why, though, look a gift horse in the mouth? A come is a come is a come.

I'm determined, though, to let this happen uncluttered by fantasies. I've had quite enough, for the moment, of both Salinas brothers, in reality and in make-believe. I came to South American hoping to try and get my life together, not complicate it with the baggage of a couple of feuding siblings whose relationship might well have Freud scratching his head in dismay.

There's always Cary Blight by way of let's-have-sex-in-my-imagination. Nice guy. Surely, he's a better choice for fucking and sucking in my daydreams than the other men presently in my life.

There was a time when I didn't employ fantasies to get off. Just a simple mindless grab of my cock, rapid beat-off, quick clean up, and a speedy get dressed. That ended when I decided I was eventually going to make it with a man, perhaps by way of preparation for that upcoming (pun intended) event.

I lather. I rinse. I lean against the cool shower-stall tiles and shift my body so that ...

"Ohhhhhh, yes!"

I've already been spray-primed far enough so that it's not going to take much longer to add my spermal spurts to the deluge.

I pinch my nipples which are swollen nubs. I squeeze harder, actually grimacing with the pain that's surprisingly — or maybe not — when combined with what's happening to my cock — masochistically pleasurable.

"Okay, Cary." I'm unable to help myself. He's just too damned cute not to invite on in.

Kyle tries to push his way on in, too, but I consciously keep him at bay. Don't need him, he's a bully. Don't need Jeremy, he's too needy.

My hands slide my chest and belly; they meet in parenthesis of my boner and balls. I massage my nuts, in their wet sac, and grind my ass against the wall.

I reach for the bar of soap I'd put back into its wall niche. I soap my hands, return the soap to its tray, and return my hands to my scrotum and testicles.

Any play of my hands for too long at my crotch will wash away all their lather, but a couple of fingers, quickly slid beneath and behind my hanging gonads, are protected from the spray by scrotal overhang and remain slick during their sensuous journey up the wet crease of my ass to my butt's pucker.

"Want to finger-fuck me while you suck my dick, Kyle?" Yeah, I say *Kyle,* despite all of my efforts not to. Fuck it!

That said, would I, in fact, like to fuck Kyle? Would I like Kyle to fuck me?

"Jesus, William, get a grip!" I push one of my strategically placed fingers into my asshole to its second knuckle and wonder if, by the way I'm standing, I can manage a prostate massage.

"You up to screwing this virgin's virgin ass, Kyle?" He'd refused the chance in my dream. Stupid fuck that he is! My ass, tight around my plugging finger, is snug enough to give even a pro at fucking, like Kyle, a run for his money. "You afraid of just how much you'll enjoy exploring my un-chartered anal territory, buddy?"

My waist bends, in order for me to poke my finger deeper up my ass. The move succeeds in letting my finger reach and poke my prostate.

"Ohhhh, baby!"

On the negative, I've put my hard dick into one of the few positions that take it out of the spray.

Instead of pulling out my finger and fucking my cock back into the deluge, I grab my dick with my free hand and start pumping like sixty. If there's not much soap left on the hand that's doing the beating, wet skin against wet skin provides friction that all the more quickly has me on the verge of exploding my nuts.

"Fuck me harder, bully-boy Kyle!" I no longer care that I've added him to the mix, even when I'd promised myself I wasn't.

It's not as if he's *really* here in the shower with me, doing what I imagining him doing.

Truth admitted, Kyle is handsome as hell. He has just the kind of masculine good looks that, from the get-go, I've found a turn on. Jeremy's looks are too perfect. Cary's looks are fantastic, but they're nothing compared to the way Kyle's dark hair hangs on his forehead, the way Kyle's dimple concaves his cheek, the way Kyle's chin cleft catches a shadow, by the way Kyle's silky curls appear at the neckline of his unbuttoned shirt, by …

"Ohhhh, Kyle, it could be so very good between us, if only there *could* be anything between us." My hand movements become speedier along the length of my priming prick.

For a moment, I surrender to the make-believe that sex with Kyle is possible … that he wouldn't use it to advantage what he wants from me ,and I'm not talking his wanting my cherry … that there would be no repercussions … that I've somehow found the one true man in my life to whom I'm ready, willing, and able to turn over, for ravaging, my virgin ass.

"Make me feel it!" I command and ram my finger deeper as my butt grinds to a deeper fit over all the knuckles of my finger.

My back slides the wall of the shower, my thighs filleting, my finger drilling my asshole even more. Suddenly, my cock spits cum like sixty into water again allowed its full-force splashing against the up-thrust length of my prick.

My neck arches my head back into the shower tiles, my face getting drenched by the cascades that, then flow down my neck, through the cleavage between my muscled pectorals, over and down my rippled abdominals, to waterfall on and over my exploding prick that continues to be pumped with a vigor that threatens to leave my penis raw in the aftermath.

"Damn … damn … damn!" My hand still tightly grips my dick but no longer beats it. My finger is still stuck up my ass but no longer strives to achieve deeper depths there.

Finally, my finger comes free of my butt. My hand lets go of my dick. My legs unbend to slide my back slowly up the wall.

I wash all over again, doing it quickly this time so there'll be no repeat of what's just happened — I'm running late the way it is.

Emerging from the bathroom, my mid-section and cum-depleted dick wrapped in a towel, I'm confronted by Pedro with a pushcart of breakfast.

"I heard the shower," he says. Did he hear my grunts and groans of orgasm as well?

"I suppose everyone is up?" I eye the covered trays and get a mouth-watering whiff of some of the food hidden from view.

"Sí, " Pedro confirms. "Up and gone."

"Did Jeremy say where he was going?" I suspect he's not really gone anywhere.

"No, senor. "

"And, Jeremy's brother?"

"Gone to see *Senora* Malendez."

Of course, I'm curious as to this woman in Kyle's life, but I decide not to badger the poor servant.

I'm determined, this day, to have a comprehensive talk with Jeremy and his brother. All of this bullshit between them and me has to be sorted out. There are certain questions I need answered. What's more, despite the convenience and decided advantages of my present luxurious surroundings, I've decided to find someplace else to stay. Let these two brothers act out without drawing me into their ongoing drama.

Pedro leaves, and I sit down to attack my late breakfast. No guinea pig on the menu, this morning. I'm delighted with real-pork sausage and scrambled eggs. The hot chocolate is especially delicious.

I finish eating.

I choose a pair of jeans and a sweat shirt from my limited wardrobe. Kyle might dress for supper, but he surely doesn't go formal for breakfast or lunch. Besides, I want to do a bit of exploring which definitely doesn't call for a suit and tie.

I go downstairs and spot two servants scuttle in the opposite direction, as if I carry the plague. They're shy or have received instructions to steer clear.

I head for the front door, having decided not to do any snooping in the main house. I have to admit, though, that it's mighty tempting to go knocking on closed doors to see if Jeremy is again locked up behind one in the absence of his brother.

The outside greets me with a glare of warm sunshine that momentarily blinds.

Belatedly, but before tripping over her, I realize there's an attractive young girl sitting the front steps. She has dark hair, dark eyes, and the kind of sultry beauty that will one day have men at her feet.

"Hi," I say. "I'm William."

"I know," she says. "You're father's friend."

"That would depend upon who your father is. I'm new around here, and I definitely don't have the family genealogy straight." Speaking of straight, that she has a father in residence may well indicate that at least one of my hosts is straight or bisexual. I can't help wondering which Salinas it is.

"Uncle Kyle says you're daddy's friend," she identifies Jeremy as her father, unless there are other Salinas brothers (or sisters) lurking somewhere in the woodwork.

In a moment of remembrance of Kyle's rundown of whom owned what percentage of the property in question, I suddenly suspect that... "I'll bet you're Jenny."

"Did father tell you about me?" She shifts several metal jacks, laid out on the concrete before her.

"Actually, I think it was your Uncle Kyle who mentioned you."

"My father doesn't talk much about me," she says. The small rubber ball, off to one side, slips the concrete, seemingly of its own accord, and bounces the steps to a jarring stop on the lawn. Jenny makes no move to retrieve it.

She frowns and gives the decided impression that she's not a very happy little girl, at least not at the moment.

"Do you happen to know where your daddy has gone this morning, honey?" I feel sneaky in giving the child the third degree when I've not been up to pressing Pedro for the answer.

She shrugs and uses one finger to edge one of the metal asterisks off the edge of the top step; she watches it drop.

"Are you going to sell out to my father?" she asks.

Her question surprises me, maybe because grown-up business doesn't seem something that should interest someone so young.

"Actually, I think that I am." I expect the revelation to cheer her up, as it did her father. Quite to the contrary, the corners of her mouth droop even farther.

She gets to her feet and literally screams at the top of her lungs, "You're an awful man, and I hate you!"

She rushes by me and into the house. Immediately, I turn but see no sign of her.

I see the animal skins on hardwood floors. I see the large walk-in fireplace that takes up much of one wall. I see the stairway to upstairs right wing. I see the mirroring stairway to the left wing within the tree. I see the leather-upholstered furniture, the numerous small tables with large bowls and vases overflowing flowers. No sign of the girl.

I turn back to the outside and its encompassing sunshine, pulling the door closed behind me. I pick up Jenny's discarded ball. I position her playthings to one side of the porch so no one will break a neck on them upon entering or exiting the building.

I have several alternatives as far as exploring the grounds. There's a straight-line stroll down the lawn to the lip of the far jungle. That's out, because I don't know what kind of wild animals exist in that underbrush that extends all of the way from the estate to the airport.

I can go to the right. There's more lawn, there, beyond which is an apparently extensive flower garden. I can make out one hedge trimmed into the likeness of a stag, another into some kind of large cat. There are streaks of blue, orange, pink, vermilion, indicating flower beds in a riot of bloom. There is water spurting higher than several banks of shrubbery surrounding it; obviously some kind of fountain. Somewhere in the same direction, there's the garage.

While I'm drawn to the fragrant display of color, I decide to go left.

I walk parallel to the front of the house. The cut lawn is soft and springy beneath my feet.

I focus on the roar of the cataracts. Surprisingly, I've only really become aware of it by concentrating on it. It's weird how my senses have adapted to the racket is such a short time. The noise certainly hasn't declined in intensity. I've just been somehow able to mute it mentally, but now that I'm willing to devote more attention to the sounds of this superb natural wonder, the volume goes up. It gets really loud when I emerge from behind the buffer offered by the massive width of the house.

I angle toward the edge of the chasm. I'm engulfed in additional decibels of intense noise from the triumph of gravity over millions of tons of water slipping the opposite escarpment. Beneath me, sound waves vibrate the rocks and send itchy sensations up through the soles of my feet.

As I get closer to the lip of the precipice, the air is even more substantially cooled by a fine mist that turns needle-like against my skin.

I stop on the edge, look across the way to water as green and as the lush as the vegetation that covers those few pieces of stone somehow defying complete erosion. A distinct fascination pulls my attention, along with the water ... down, down, down ... to the depths, lost in thick spray.

I don't know exactly what I feel at that moment. It's similar to the queasiness I experience when standing in all high places, yet something more. There's awesomeness to the sight on its own merits. The sheer energy at work is staggering. Minute by minute, hour by hour, day by day, week by week, month by month, year by year, water disappears over the brink and splatters rocks below. For how long has it continued, up until now? What did the first primitive native think when he stumbled out of the jungle to see all these powerful forces of nature in motion? Encased as I am within a few generations of civilized existence, I'm certainly still awe-struck by the sheer wonder of what's before me.

My gaze slides the upper curve of the major falls to where its sheet of seeming glass is broken by undergrowth-grown stone that splits spilling water into separate cascades.

I continue to walk away from the house, stopping now and again to admire the sunlight caught by the spray and shattered into rainbow shards.

At the end of the lawn, I'm confronted by a tall tangle of tropical underbrush that rears in a barrier as functional as any cyclone fence.

I'm prepared to turn back but see the small pathway that proceeds over the edge. The chasm no longer seems a sheer drop to its depths but more a steep angle downward and back toward the direction of the house. I decide to take the path. Why not? I'm experiencing a delicious one-with-nature euphoria and don't want to spoil it.

The ground offers firm footing, not so slippery that I don't feel secure while on it. Greenery sprouts all around. Plant life thrives in this constant humid hot-house environment.

While no huge trees have gained footholds within or on the stone, triumphant bushes are hung with long veils of trailing green-gray moss beyond which plunges the precipice and the water into it.

I look upward but can no longer see the top of the cliff. The undergrowth rooted on my right leans to the left as it grows, and forms the natural arbor through which I walk.

It becomes downright chilly.

Through some mysterious trick of acoustics, all sound actually seems, at times, on the verge of complete disappearance. I hum a tune to see if I can hear my own voice.

Myriad flowers are locked within the surrounding vegetation. Huge, multi-petal blossoms that I've never seen before, even in greenhouses, come complete with thick and decidedly phallic stamens gone puffy and fat with yellow, white, and tan pollen.

I'm so caught up by one exceptionally large blossom, dark red and shot through and through with thick pink veins that I don't see the spider web weaved across my path until I'm about in it. My sudden reaction, not only to the gossamer veil but to the grotesquely large and fat "creature" which has weaved it, is momentary paralysis. I'm but inches from bumping noses with the gross arachnid suspended in space before me.

When I do regain my ability to move, it's for a hasty about-face and an intended immediate return back the way I've come. Literally, I bump against the solidness of Kyle Salinas's inconveniently positioned muscled body.

"Damn! Sorry about that," I apologize. Or, should *he* be the one apologizing *to me?*

Suddenly, I'm fearful that our unexpected meet-up has propelled me back in the spider's direction. I turn back for a quick glimpse of the web that's still intact but now empty.

This doesn't mean the spider isn't still there, somewhere, or that I'm the only one who saw it.

"Actually, it's quite harmless as far as spiders go," Kyle says. "More used to entrapping insects, I doubt he (or she) would have known what to do with big-ol'-you had you stumbled on in uninvited."

"That's somehow very little consolation, thanks, anyway," I admit. Then, rather than keep to that line of embarrassing conversation, I deflect to, "I thought you were off on a hot date."

"Date?" He seems genuinely confused; maybe little Jenny had it wrong.

"*Senora* Malendez," I refresh his memory.

"Ah yes," he says. "Well, I finished early with Maria and came home to see guess-who headed down this particular pathway. Come on, William, surely, you've not come this far only to miss the piece de resistance just a few steps farther down? If we stoop low, we can limbo right on under the web without even disturbing it or its owner." He points to where sparse anchoring strings of silk hold one corner of the woven structure to bordering shrubbery.

He performs the required walk-through, turning back to me still on the other side.

Against my better judgment, wishing I wasn't egged on by my desire that he not think me a complete chicken-shit, I follow after, shivering all of the damned way.

"See!" he says. "Obstacles are just things to overcome."

I don't ask him to definite what obstacles, other than this one, to which he may refer.

Quickly, the trail grows wide enough so that we can walk it side by side. Its eventual conclusion is an additional widening onto a sizable slab of blue-black rock. The vegetation retreats as I step onto the fantastic natural platform. My senses are assaulted by the roar, the splatter, and the smell of static electricity.

Contradictory to my impression atop the gorge, the chasm walls don't ever drop perpendicular to the riverbed. They slant downward like the arms of a giant "V". The water rolls the far arm like a deluge along the cemented sloped front of a large dam. Liquid splashes loud and hard in the V's crotch. Where Kyle and I stand, there's spray and an occasional rhythmic pulse of water that sloshes from the river to bathe part of the black rock slab — only to drain away before it reaches our feet.

Kyle taps my shoulder and points toward the outer lip of the flat stone. He says something lost in the din. I shake my head and go through a pantomime of pointing at my ears and, then, at the water. He gets the idea and fastens his fingers gently into my shoulder to edge me closer to one side. There's a small crease in the cliff face. When we wedge ourselves into it, we're partially shielded from the elements, and from their sounds.

There isn't much room in which to manipulate. My back is against rock, and Kyle stands so close that we're actually touching. I'm acutely aware of the steamy warmth of his body and the expansions and contractions of his muscled chest as he breathes.

He puts his hands to the rock above and just behind me. He leans in closer. The hard length of him increases its pressure against me. I have a close up view of the curling mass of black hair that sprouts from the breach of his open shirt collar. It, like his head hair, is damp and glossy with moisture. The material of his shirt is so wet it's transparent and clings sensuously to the flesh and muscle beneath it. I can actually see the dark brown of his nipples.

His lips are up close to my ear; his breath is hot.

Unsure as to where I should put my hands, I gently rest them on his waist — solid bulk — no fat.

His mouth moves against my earlobe. It sounds as if he says, "William, William."

My hands helplessly slide his flanks. My fingertips discover the deep groove that runs the center of his back. There are rope-like ridges of muscle where his large neck anchors his impressive shoulders.

His head tilts slightly. His mouth opens. The tip of his tongue darts to further dampen his already mist-glossed lips. His teeth are white beyond coral-tinted lips.

He's going to kiss me. My mouth goes partially slack in preparation and opens in anticipation of the pressure his lips will surely deliver. I shut my eyes, tilt my head slightly to better align with his, and wait for the moment to happen.

My first man-on-man kiss doesn't disappoint. His lips touch mine, press hard. His mouth slowly works my lips wider. His hands drop from the rock, his arms encircling me. His chest and belly mate even more securely with mine. His cock is hard in his pants and battles for position between us and beside my hard dick, the latter standing straight-arrow within my soaked trousers and under shorts.

I'm crushed by his strength. I go limp against him, except for my cock which goes stiffer.

As much as I enjoy the uniqueness of this long-to-achieve and long-anticipated man-lips-to-my-lips moment -and I do enjoy it, having finally succumbed to the temptation of being kissed by another man- I refuse to be caught up in the sheer wonder of it. Already, I have second thoughts. What, after all, am I doing? Unless I actually plan to go farther, I'm playing the tease, and it's not a role in which I'm comfortable.

What, after all, about Jeremy? There's a battle going on between the two half-brothers, and I'm not sure I want to give Kyle any false ideas that my loyalty lies anywhere than with Jeremy. I might not know all of the facts; those I do know lead me to believe that Jeremy is being bullied by his stronger half-brother. It won't do to let Kyle think that he now has some kind of power over me — even a seductive one, purely based on mutual lust. I have no doubt but that he'll attempt to put any such assumed advantage to his benefit.

I break the kiss. His face lingers close, as if in eager anticipation of another.

My hands move from his back to his chest. My splayed palms feel the delineation of his muscled pectorals as I push, well aware of his obvious unwillingness to budge. If he thinks I've completely succumbed to his charms, he has quite another think coming.

Maybe at another time, another place, I wouldn't cut this enjoyable little interlude short. Under the present circumstances, though…

He *is* going to try and kiss me again. I read it in his eyes. I feel it in the muscle tension relayed from his body through my fingertips. No sense denying that receiving another kiss from him is an exciting temptation, after the pleasure of the first one, especially as I've never met a man to whom I've been quite so physically attracted. However, pure unadulterated lust, which is very likely what I'm experiencing, albeit for the very first time with a man, makes any second kiss, here and now, entirely out of the question.

"I'm cold!" I say loud enough for him to hear above the roar of the water. In emphasis, I provide a shiver that's not all feigned.

His expression is priceless, rejection having obviously taken him by complete surprise. Someone like Kyle probably isn't used to having men or women turn him away, especially after such mutually shared all-around enjoyable preliminaries.

"Cold!" I repeat. I'm still capable of very little movement. Stone is to my rear; Kyle blocks my forward momentum. My hands give him another firm push, yet he's reluctant to move.

I tell myself to remain calm, cool, and collected. After all, I have something to my advantage that any other man, so cornered by Kyle Salinas, wouldn't have. It's something Kyle wants more than me or my body. It's my ten percent of *The Cataracts*. So, I'm confident he won't press his advantage, here and now, and risk alienating me any more than I possibly already am.

As predicted, he lets me by. I brush his body before being hit full-force by the spray from which he's concealed me.

I move through the wet, drenched, and manage the shelter of the shrubbery-shielded pathway.

I turn and wait for Kyle to join me. I smile. There's no sense letting him think I've had a miserable time when I haven't.

"I never did figure out just what you were trying to point out to me out there," I say, no embarrassing mention of our kiss and my rejection of a second.

He says something and, then, uses sign language to let me know it would be easier to talk a little farther back up the trail.

We walk until the roar dims miraculously to a level more easily overridden by our voices without our screaming at the top of our lungs.

"I was pointing out where they found her," he says.

"Found who?"

"Jeremy's mother." He gives me a decidedly curious look that, sure as hell, denotes his disbelief that I'm as ignorant as I pretend. "Surely, Jeremy told you his mother was a suicide."

CHAPTER FIVE

It's almost eight p.m.

I open the door and step into the hallway. I go downstairs and into the hallway leading to a dining room that's empty. The table isn't set.

I'm wondering if Kyle has decided to avoid all additional talk of Jeremy's mother, after having gone completely silent on the subject, at the bottom of the gorge, when it finally struck him that I hadn't a clue.

"Sorry I'm late," he surprises me from behind.

His smile is friendly and warm. He wears a black brocade dinner jacket with tuxedo trousers. His shirt is white, a run of scalloped ruffles flow the total length between his jacket lapels. A butterfly bow tie, black, is fastened at his neck. Ruffled shirt cuffs exhibit exquisite gold cufflinks. He looks very attractive and well turned-out, indeed.

"We seem to be early," I say. "This restaurant apparently isn't yet open."

"Actually, I've made reservations elsewhere. I thought you might enjoy dining in the tree house this evening."

He leads me out of the corridor and up the stairway. *Tree house* is as much a misnomer as de Veer *farm*. It looks nothing like the stereotypical same-name structures erected in backyard trees by fathers out to please their kids. This massive structure is a series of architectural marvels that helix the main trunk and migrate the branches.

"*Ficus Benghalensis,*" Kyle says; I turn to him, uncertain what he's saying. "The tree," he clarifies, "is a banyan. Somewhat of a mystery how it got here, considering it's a native to India. While planted extensively around the world, it only grows wild in the Lower Himalayas and Deccan Hills. However this one got here, somehow, and thrives. The main trunk is forty feet in circumference, and there are over two-hundred additional trunks ranging from six to ten feet in diameter."

We're in a semi-circle room, its inner curve holds to the main trunk, its outer curve is a wall of glass looking out on the chasm, although all I see, at the moment, is Kyle and my reflections.

By one section of the window, there's a small table set for two, on which a low bowl overflows with large creamy orchids that possibly account for the pleasant smell all around us. A large pale-white (scented?) candle, in its exquisitely worked crystal holder, burns next to the flower arrangement and casts an angelic nimbus of flickering light throughout its commandeered portion of the room.

"Vodka martini?" Kyle motions me into one of the chairs at the table. "Of course, you can ask for anything, but vodka martinis are my specialty."

"Love one."

He mixes drinks at a small bar set-up. He does so with expertise and assurance. Obviously, he's a man, at least at the moment, within his element.

He brings our drinks to the table and sits down across from me. Simultaneously, all lights in the room, save that of the candle, go out.

He's even more handsome in candlelight, his eyes deep pools of velvety violet.

He raises his glass…

"To handsome William." His dimple sinks deeper. His teeth are exceptionally white in his tanned face. His ebony hair is sexily rumpled. Undeniably, I want to run my fingers through it and achieve some better semblance of order.

"To solutions," I propose in alternative.

"You really don't think I'm putting forth much effort to settle the problems here, do you, William?" he asks, but only after having sipped from his glass. "What's more, you still view me as the villain of this piece, yes?"

"I merely think it's impossible to keep Jeremy locked in his room forever," I say. It would be so much easier to avoid this subject, just enjoy the company, the wine, the moment.

In a way, the setting is too perfect, the man across from me too attractive — to be real.

"Hopefully, I won't have to keep Jeremy locked up forever." Kyle is no long smiling but his dimple is still evident within the center of his right cheek.

"Each day you do keep him locked up only makes things more difficult between you, don't you think?"

"Nothing would make me happier than having him out and gone." His purple eyes look into mine intently. "Jeremy does so hate it here. I know that. Despite what you both may think, I'm not in the least sadistically pleased by the part I'm playing in keeping him locked up here like the family idiot no one likes to talk about, or even likes to admit exists. Unfortunately, he leaves me little choice. The few times I've allowed him some slack, he's moved with unparalleled swiftness to take unfair advantage. He's not without his charm, as I'm sure you know. I'm not always immune to that charm, either; much to my chagrin. The last time he convinced me he was adjusting, I found myself stranded in the middle of nowhere with a sabotaged Jeep, you arriving at the airport. If I hadn't commandeered transportation from one poor local who just happened by, I'd probably be holed up here, now, with an arsenal, defending the fortress from its new owners, hotel moguls, whose metal-jawed bulldozers have quickly arrived in the guise of bringing progress to Iguassu."

"Do you keep Jenny locked up, too?"

His smile is unexpected.

"I understand you two met," he says. "It'll be Jeremy who'll insist she apologize to you for being rude. I'm too sympathetic to her reasoning to insist she come to you with bowed head to eat humble pie."

"She, no more than you, then, eager for her father to gain a majority of *The Cataracts*?"

"Like I, born here." His answer to my question.

"Jeremy born …?"

"Capri. Raised there and in a bevy of cosmopolitan locales, boarding school in Switzerland, until the money ran out. He didn't even see *The Cataracts* until the bottom fell out of our father's finances. When that happened, the only things left being this house and a few parcels of land in Paraguay, everyone ended up here. Certainly, my father wasn't pleased to be back. When my mother died, he'd headed on off, leaving *The Cataracts* and me, because we reminded him too much of her. He met Deidre in London, married her in Paris, and fathered Jeremy on Capri. None of that trio was able to cope with being here. Two of them are dead, possibly as a result. Who knows just how long Jeremy is going to last?"

He opens the bottle of white wine brought to the table in a sterling champagne bucket by our server. He fills our glasses.

We drink and eat in relative silence until the next course arrives.

"It's Peruvian," he says and forks a piece of meat in his plate. "*Chicharrones.* Small pieces of meat from a pig's ribs fried with ground garlic."

"Really good," I say and mean it.

"You know …" he says a short time later, placing his fork and knife across the top edge of his plate in signal of being finished despite not having eaten all his food. He reaches for the wine bottle and slowly refills our glasses. "…my brother is really far cleverer than I sometimes give him credit for. He has somehow managed to manipulate me into a position — or, even more skillfully managed to let me manipulate myself into the position — where I must dredge up the family skeletons. All of which is going to make him sound the martyr. You're sure he didn't tell you about his mother?"

"Only that he doesn't want to end up like she did." I use the prongs of my fork to shift my mashed potatoes a fraction of an inch to the left.

Kyle pyramids his index fingers against his full lower lip. "Whatever, it's going to sound as if Jeremy is Cinderfella and I'm his wicked half-brother. So, I might as well make the leap and tell you that my dear, admittedly beautiful, stepmother was a lush, pure and simple. No matter how many times Jeremy tries to convince himself and others that she was driven to insanity and suicide by the roar of the cataracts, it has always been more logically assumed that she just got drunk one evening and fell off the balcony."

"Suicide or drunken tumble, no wonder Jeremy doesn't like it here."

Kyle drains the last of the wine from his glass.

"Jeremy doesn't think that I feel for his predicament," Kyle says and rolls the stem of his empty glass back and forth between his thumb and forefinger. "In truth, though, I do feel for him. I'd do most anything to be able to tell him to go back to the good times in Rome, in Zurich, in London. After all, it was never my intention that my father, and Jeremy, and Deidre end up here. Blame father. Blame bad grain futures. Blame the collapse of a key mine shaft in South Africa. Blame an investment broker who panicked at the wrong time and bought when he should have sold. I'm not to blame and refuse to give up what's most important to me just because Jeremy has been forced by circumstances to give up what's most important to him."

It doesn't take a diviner to see that Kyle loves this place, probably even more than Jeremy hates it.

"I was born here," he says. "I've lived here all of my life. It's a good place, William. It has fresh air, space to live without feeling cramped and confined. It has lots of good people who won't survive some multi-million dollar hotel plopped down right in the middle of their banana-leaf huts just so drunken tourists can gawk at empty beer cans riding the falls."

I don't want Kyle to think I'm swayed to his way of thinking, by the setting, by the wine, by the moment — even if that possibly is becoming more and more the case.

"Of course, you and I see from where Jeremy is coming," Kyle says. "However, to save you from having to make a decision either way, I'm merely going to keep you from making a decision in Jeremy's favor by keeping you separated from him for as long as your stay here. As soon as you leave, the sooner Jeremy will, again, have more rope to play with."

"That's not *really* solving anything, you know. All it does is delay the inevitable. Do you think any of this will end if I go home tomorrow?"

"I'd be content just to have you keep out of it," he says and leans across the table toward me. His purple eyes reflect the flickering candle flame. "I need time. You, here, with your ten percent dangling in front of Jeremy like bloody carcass before a carnivore, has my half-brother blinded by prospects of again having some of the money we once had."

Outside, the cataracts become suddenly and spectacularly illuminated by hundreds of strategically placed and triggered spotlights.

Immediately, I'm caught up in the sight now visible beyond the glass. It seems unbelievable that I had, but minutes before, been eating and drinking, here, carrying on a conversation, while all of that natural wonder had existed just beyond the glass, concealed from me by soundproofing and darkness.

Cataract after cataract foams. Water roils white with trapped air bubbles as it drops from one level ... to another ... to another. Big and small waterfalls cascade amid mist turned to countless rainbows by the artificial lighting.

Huge leaves reach out and move in the spray to sample and grow lusher with the nourishment they derive from the water. Shrubbery, as if sweating, glistens with moisture.

I feel very much like God looking down on all creation, in close affinity with each and everything I see.

I turn to admit to Kyle that, yes, I *do* understand how he can fight so hard to save all of this wonder from exploitation.

Kyle, though, is gone.

WET SHEETS

LAURA BAUMBACH

"You're barely a handful. I bet your whole ass will fit in the palm of one of my hands."

Choosing not to comment, Nicholas hit the bed hard. He bounced twice and ended up flat on his back, legs sprawled, eager cock jutting straight and high in the air. The rough texture of the woven bedspread scraped his naked ass and shoulders, raising a warm tingle across his skin.

It wasn't his bed, wasn't his bedroom. Not one of the lotion bottles or creams on the bedside table looked familiar, though he could guess what they were used for. The he-man he was with didn't strike him as a skin care prima donna.

The bright afternoon sunlight streaming through the bedroom windows gave the expansive, masculine, tidy space a cheery, surreal setting.

He didn't even know the name of the person the room belonged to. All he knew was he had been hot and horny and in the mood for something different. He was tired of working a month long string of late hours and no days off at the bookstore he managed.

The killer schedule left him little energy for anything else. The most enthusiasm he could work up by the weekend was wasted on boring Friday nights spent watching TV capped by restless Saturday nights wasted cruising bars or talking with the same people he'd seen all week at work. He had needed to shake things up a little.

So here he was, shaking. Literally.

The owner of the bed, long limbed and thickly muscled, slowly began to crawl onto the mattress. Nicholas felt the bed dip, the box springs giving a faint creak of protest against the added weight.

"Shit, you look small in my bed. You, not your cock. That looks delicious, especially right now."

As if to prove his point, the man rubbed his clean-shaven, strong Scandinavian-featured face appreciatively on Nicholas's dick. Unseen stubble grated lightly over his cock's head. Nicholas gasped and jerked, but there was nowhere to go, no escape from the faintly abrasive pleasure.

Beneath him the plush king-size mattress cradled him in a nest of rough woven spreads, sheets and dense pillows. Above he was held in place by the mass of advancing raw sex appeal he'd impulsively said yes to five minutes after locking eyes on the handsome man.

Ten minutes later he was pinned between the man's powerful thighs and tree limb sized arms.

Just where Nicholas wanted to be.

God, this guy was gorgeous, glorious and strong like a tall oak tree or Old World Viking come to life. Over six foot five, the man had shoulders that were almost twice as wide as Nicholas's, an abundance of well-formed muscle bound tightly to long bones by smooth, golden-hued skin that boasted a fairly dense carpet of curly hair a shade darker than the tanned flesh it grew from.

"Small, compact. Exactly the way I like. Cute, too, real cute."

The intensity of the guy's needy stare shot a jolt of excitement up Nicholas's spine so intense he knew he'd shivered. He could feel his own shimmy of anticipation and a sudden rise in body heat transmitted across every square inch where their skin touched.

The guy froze in his slow crawl up Nicholas's body, his expression stunned but pleased. "Did you just shudder for me?"

"Yeah, yeah. Sorry." Chuckling softly, Nicholas wanted to bite his tongue to keep from sounding so nervous and young. "You've got me hard and ready, and I don't even know your name."

"Don't be sorry. I like it. My name's Erp." His expression became self-effacing, his half-smile wry and thoroughly endearing to Nicholas. "It's a family name. Swedish. It means big, strong, courageous. Son of a Norse hero no one outside of Sweden ever heard of."

He teasingly flexed a bicep and struck the best facsimile of a muscleman pose he could without moving more than one arm, making a show of sucking in his already flat abdomen and tightening his entire impressive frame briefly. "My parents had... expectations about my size."

He held the pose for about three seconds before he dropped his arm back down to brace himself over Nicholas's torso, dipping his head to lick over each taut nipple on Nicholas's chest. Apparently he wasn't a man that could be distracted from his main objective for long.

Nicholas pried his fingers out of the grip he had on the bedspread to let his hands wander over Erp's shoulders and chest, tweaking swollen teats and massaging bands of hard flesh. Power rippled under his touch with each sexy, stalking inch Erp advanced up his body. It was intoxicating.

"I think you've met those expectations and then some, Erp." His lips were so dry he could barely get the words out. "I'm Nicholas. And you are *hot*."

"If anyone is hot here, it's you, Nicky." Erp gaze raked over Nicholas's body, one hand sliding along the same path.

"Nicholas."

Just the intensity of it set Nicholas's skin burning and his cock weeping.

"Nah. That's too long. Nicky fits you better."

He wanted to explode from the frustration of waiting for the man to do more than touch him.

"I can't believe I've never seen you before. We live in the same neighborhood."

He could barely keep focused on the conversation but Erp apparently liked small talk before sex. Not that Nicholas picked up strangers often, but it was kind of comforting not to have 'hit and run' sex for a change. "Guess today was just fate, Erp. I'm not going to complain. I'm just glad I needed groceries."

He'd always wanted to be with a huge hunk of a lover, but something had always made him retreat when the chance presented itself before this. The reasons were many—fear of being overpowered, fear of being hurt, fear of having his first time doing something besides a quick blow job and some heavy petting being too much for him to handle with an average sized guy, let alone a giant.

He didn't know why, but he trusted Erp from the moment the man had smiled at him in the checkout line. A casual conversation in the parking lot had led to an exchange of cell numbers, which quickly escalated into Nicholas helping Erp take his groceries home. Groceries that had been dropped by the front door and long forgotten.

The bed shifted again as Erp sat back on his hunches, his tight ass snuggling down on Nicholas's legs, his large square hands spread open on bunched thighs. His fingers were long and thick, just like his cock. His deep bronze dick curved up, swollen in a slight arch so complete that the head touched Erp's lower belly. It looked like a massive handle, one Nicholas longed to reach out and grab. He wanted to pull Erp down with it, covering himself with a blanket of hot, sweaty manflesh. Talk about fantasies!

Instead, Nicholas licked dry lips and forced his gaze up to meet Erp's smoldering, hungry stare. His own cock flexed, swelling impossibly harder, shedding glistening beads of cream that oozed out his tiny slit.

He gasped as Erp suddenly wiped off the gathering bead with a fingertip. He felt his lungs momentarily freeze when his lover scooped the cum from his fingertip with a broad sweep of his tongue.

No one had ever tasted him like that before. Erp was not only the physical man of his dreams but an uninhibited one as well. The sight made Nicholas's stomach roll with excitement, the erotic gesture so intimate, so unexpected.

A heady smile tugged at Erp's lips as he savored the taste. "Like cream inside an éclair." The smile turned voracious. "Does the rest of you taste this good?"

Sitting on Nicholas's knees, Erp was perfectly positioned so when he leaned over his long frame would match Nicholas's shorter height. Erp planted his hands on the bed by Nicholas's shoulders and stared down, his gaze lustful and dark, his tone husky, dripping with sexual desire. "I suddenly feel like a big hungry lion pouncing on a young gazelle."

Nicholas felt a surge of queasiness—need mixed with a measure of fear. His gaze scanned over Erp's beefy arms and muscular chest. He could feel the power in the man's thighs where they pressed his own lean legs together. This man was twice his size, three times as powerful. Not that now was the time to worry about it but what if Nicholas didn't want to do something Erp did?

Suddenly one of those big square hands touched his chin, titling his face so their eyes meet. "You look nervous. Don't be. I know to take it easy. Hardly any of my partners have been as strong as I am. I won't break you. Promise."

The touch was light, undemanding. Erp's expression had lost a bit of the predatory look. Concern made the tiny, tanned wrinkles at the corners of his eyes suddenly more noticeable, attractively so. His voice was still husky with need but constrained. Erp didn't strike Nicholas as the type of man who lost control easily. It probably took a lot of discipline, physical and mental, to build that he-man body.

With nothing more than instinct to go on, Nicholas believed him. "I'm okay. Just... anxious." Like hell he was going to let the guy know how terrified he was. He wanted this and nothing was going to stop him now.

"I hear you. I was like that at your age." The hand fell away from his face to settle on his chest, the blunt finger delicately tracing the outer ring of one of his nipples. The effect was immediate. His cock jumped and his mouth went dry. "I'm thirty. What are you? Twenty?"

He felt a flush of heat travel from his face all the way to his navel. "*Twenty-three.* It's just... This was kind of an impulse thing. I'm—I'm a little nervous."

"I can see that." Erp smiled and some of Nicholas's nervousness drained away. "Kind of refreshing. Cute. Don't see that much these days." Erp leaned down and kissed Nicholas's cheek, then the other one, a light, teasing caress of lips brushed over sensitive skin. "You just lay back and let me play. You can jump in any time once you're less nervous." A quick lick followed by sharp nip stung the tip of his chin. "Let me know if I get it right."

Warm, wet lips moved across his cheek, down his neck to his chest, lingering in all the right places. By the time they had fastened to one of Nicholas's aching nipples, his whole body was flushed, vibrating with need. His limbs jerked with faint spasms, fighting off the desire to grab Erp by his splendid cock and beg him to fuck him, to be his first.

Nicholas grabbed at Erp, one hand twisting through the thick honey blond hair on Erp's head while the other rubbed its fisted knuckles up and down Erp's arched spine and shoulders. Breath hissed out between his teeth. Begging words of encouragement stuck to the tip of his tongue, held back by the desire not to look too desperate or naïve.

Warmth flowed over his belly, touching hip and thigh in a heavy caress as Erp explored his skin on a tactile quest that ended at his cock. Nicholas kept from crying out with relief but he couldn't stop his hips from rising up to meet the first delicious down stroke of Erp's tightly fisted hand. When a rough palm polished the tip on the up stroke and a thumb teased the flared edge of the head, his vision blurred.

"Must have done something right. I just heard you sigh." The words were spoken against his parted lips, his swollen, wet teat abandoned. Nicholas had to swallow hard to find his voice.

"Christ, yeah. Everything you do is *right*." The air smelled of sweat, aftershave and spicy soap. The faint scent of lotion wafted off the bedside stand. Erp's body felt silky smooth and rock hard, all rippling muscle and restrained power. Just the touch of the man's skin was intoxicating. When it touched and then pulled away from Nicholas's own flushed body, a sensation like static electricity buzzed along Nicholas's nerves.

Another stroke and twirl of his cock and Nicholas found those forbidden words he'd held back earlier. "I-I want you to fuck me. Now. Please."

Begging, damn. He didn't even know he could do that. Being this close to the he-man from his best wet dreams was making him do things he'd never done with another guy. Fucking, begging, Christ, what was next? Cutsie nicknames?

"Soon, babycheeks, soon. I like to work up to the big connection, especially with you. Your waist fits in my hand. You're so small. I want to work *you* up to needing it, not just wanting it, Nicky."

Okay, fucking, begging, teasing, and not one but two cutsie nicknames. This had to be a dream. "I need it. Now, Erp. Honest."

"You just think you do. You'll need it more soon. Trust me." With that, Erp slid his whole bruiser body further down Nicholas's legs until he could pull Nicholas's legs out from under him. He silently urged Nicholas to bend his knees and spread his thighs while Erp grabbed Nicholas's hips, raising Nicholas's ass in the air.

Broad shoulders supporting most of his body's weight, Nicholas's cock bobbed in front of Erp's face, dark pink, long and slender, like an offered peppermint stick. A tantalizing candy the other man couldn't resist.

Erp nudged Nicholas's legs back and apart with a touch of his cheek, the fine stubble leaving patches of prickling heat behind.

Nicholas's thigh trembled with the strain of trying to hold them up until he finally gave in and let them fall to the sides, calves resting on Erp's bulky upper arms and shoulders. He gasped and shuddered as the beard stubble burn washed over his exposed perineum and balls, the shudder melting into a sustained quiver as his already tightening sac was licked and tasted. Each ball was sucked into Erp's mouth, tongued and rolled before being released. The cooler air of the room cooled the lingering moisture left behind. Nicholas could feel his sac draw up and harden. The sensation sent a fissure of pleasure through his belly that shot into his ass and dick, both begging for immediate attention.

He watched the tip of Erp's tongue protrude from between his lips as he bent down and kissed the swollen head of Nicholas's cock. Nicholas jerked. Erp's lips closed over the leaking knob and he sucked gently.

Nicholas's cock disappeared into Erp's mouth, the shaft rigid, the thrill of the teasing vacuum heightening his arousal. Hammer blows of excitement pounded through him. He gasped and moaned. Erp's teeth closed gently on the hard roll of flesh while his tongue played with the tender slit. Hands milked his shaft, massaging and stroking until Nicholas didn't know what sensation to concentrate on first.

Nicholas felt the gathering pre-orgasmic knot form in his belly. His knees jerked and his buttocks clenched. Erp's bobbing head followed each erratic movement, never breaking rhythm. Nicholas felt himself spiraling toward climax but before he hit the point of no return, Erp released his dick and lowered his hips to the bed.

Nicholas sighed, one hand on his chest to measure the pounding of his heart. He just about lost it in under five minutes like an inexperienced adolescent. He'd utter an apology to Erp if he could talk. He studied Erp's face, looking for signs of mockery. All he saw was a lust and desire that matched his own.

"You okay, Nicky? Still with me, baby? We want to make this last, right?" A warm, comforting hand rubbed his belly.

Okay. He could play this game. He could hold out until Erp wanted it as badly as he did. He'd make this awesome he-man Viking God claim his little virgin ass if it was the last thing he did.

"Yeah. I'm here. Just barely."

"We need to take it down a notch. Make it last."

"Don't slow down on my account." Nicholas stroked his cock to demonstrate how ready, willing and able he was.

"Let the burn build, baby. The blaze will be brighter when it comes." Erp grinned and pulled his hand away. "Turn over."

The command came with a playful slap to Nicholas's ass. He instinctively obeyed. Two helping hands flipped his body over. Startled at first then thrilled by the easy manhandling, Nicholas took a deep breath and settled down onto the plush sheets.

Okay. So they were going to fuck. He could do this. He was ready. Didn't he read somewhere to use something under his hips to make it easier? Nicholas grabbed a pillow and handed it back toward Erp. Erp took it but tossed it aside.

"This will feel better if you don't use that. Your spine will be straighter."

"Um, okay. If you say so."

"I do. I've done this a million times. You'll love it. The sheets get pretty wet but I like it that way." Nicholas could here the smile in his voice. Bottles rattled and the scent of lotion tainted the air. "Soggy sheets." A short snort self-depreciation smoothed a little of Nicholas's nervousness. "Must be my own personal kink."

Nicholas found the simple slick-slide of lotion being rubbed between palms sounded exciting and oddly lewd when a person was naked and face down in a strange bed. That was a new experience. At least Erp was going to use lube. Thank god. The more the better, wet sheets be damned.

The panic that had been building in his chest eased a little. But as a huge, heated weight settled over his thighs and ass, Nicholas froze, his brain hastily reexamining his choice of partners for his first time with anal intercourse. Then slick hands slid up his back and began kneading his shoulders, arms, and neck, a muscle group at a time. Nicholas groaned and melted into the bed.

"Good, huh? I knew you'd like it."

A long heavy stroke traced his spine to the curve of his ass.

"I work with my hands and they show it, but I love the feel of warm, supple skin. Your skin is soft as warm fur."

The weight on Nicholas shifted a little and warm breath caressed his shoulder and cheek. The air around him grew heavy with the smell of lotion, body heat and something earthy that reminded him of rainy days. "You like?"

Nicholas envisioned the strong, massaging fingers on his back moving lower to worm their way under his hips to find his now aching dick. The imagined slap-slide of viscous lotion and the power of the work rough hands caressing his shaft made his cock throb and his ass ache with need. His shoulders were relaxed, but his balls were growing blue. He managed to choke out a short answer. "I like." A groan escaped him. He didn't know if it was from frustration or pleasure but loosened his natural shyness in bed to whisper a suggestion. "Lower, maybe?"

"You know it, baby."

Despite his reassurances, Erp continued to knead and rub Nicholas's shoulders awhile longer. His hands were so large they felt as if they covered Nicholas's entire upper back without moving. Their heat radiated into his skin. The light friction of the massage worked the warmth deep into his body, the slight drag of Erp's work-hardened hands brought a tingle to his skin, one that worked its way into his chest, spreading out like ripples on a pond to reach all the way to his toes.

When that same tingle reached his groin, it coiled around his balls and drew them in tight. His cock ached, still swollen and needy, the sheets under him growing damper by the minute.

The shock of a chilly, slick wetness being drizzled over his skin conjured up the mental image of creamy ropes of cum shooting from Erp's cock onto his ass instead of the simple addition of lotion it really was.

With another shift in weight, Erp moved down Nicholas's legs. His palms explored Nicholas's back in small concentric circles, easing slowly over faintly prominent ribs and spine until they reached the soft globes of his quivering ass. Once there, their tempo changed, the firm rubbing rhythm now a power-filled kneading, almost a worshipping of Nicholas's flesh.

"Oh, God. Please." It was a low sigh, so pleading and needy he hoped it was lost in the mattress, but Erp's soft, pleased chuckle told him otherwise.

"There's that sigh again." Erp planted one hand on the mattress beside Nicholas's face, leaning down close to whisper, "Christ, that turns me on, Nicky." When he straightened, he left a dark, lotion-scented handprint on the spread. *Wet sheets.*

Suddenly the phrase conjured up all kinds of fantasies for Nicholas, all the different ways the two of them could create wet sheets. But that would mean more encounters like this one. Nicholas couldn't think about anything but the sensations of the here and now.

More lotion dripped onto him. It puddled at the small of his back, quickly warmed by the flush of his skin. The air carried a scent he finally recognized as aloe, earthy and soothing. Nicholas twisted his hands into the sheeting and bedspread, the fabrics already damp with his sweat.

Erp's fingers dug into his ass, kneading, gripping, and massaging. Every now and then his thumbs would slide into the crease to rub over the puckered opening of his body. His hole winked and fluttered at the attention, flirting and offering him up to whatever those teasing digits hinted at.

He felt wanton and a little dirty. Lying in broad sunlight, spread out on a stranger's bed, naked and hard—*sighing.*

But who could blame him? Erp was gorgeous. Massive compared to Nicholas's slender build and below average height, all rugged Viking conqueror. And no doubt about it, Nicholas was more than willing to be the spoils of war for Erp. Yet his voice and his expression, when Nicholas could see it, was more gentle lover than primal pillager. His touch nearly vibrated with constrained power, as if he was consciously aware of his ability to bruise and break with a simple touch.

Nicholas felt a surge of something indefinable ripple through him, something that made him imagine a safe haven. He had the sneaking suspicion it would only last while he was in Erp's company. The man's strength was like a sanctuary. Nicholas wanted to be wrapped in the man's embrace, wanted to wear this gentle giant like a cloak. He wanted to experience every inch of the he-man, wanted Erp inside of him. Now.

"I need..." He didn't know how to ask, so Nicholas pushed his ass into Erp's hands in a wordless plea. Silence answered him but the kneading didn't stop so he tried again, ignoring the bite of fingernails as he pushed to his knees. "I... want... you." He hated that his voice shook.

He stared at the handprint on the sheet, feeling the same hard palm and short thick fingers playing with his ass cheeks. The hands moved to his hips and pulled them backward so that Nicholas's ass touched his heels.

"Put your shoulders down, relax." A pillow was shoved under his nose and he obediently curled his arms around it, resting his upper torso on the cool pillowcase. His ass cheeks eased apart, exposing his hole. The cool air of the room tickled the sensitive flesh but the chill was chased away by a firm, heated touch.

Erp pushed at the tight ring of muscle, his fingertip drawing small circles, filling the puckers with a new, slicker wetness, poking the tiny portal in short stabs that inflamed Nicholas's need and did nothing to satisfy it. He shoved back, trying to capture the digit, to sink it deep inside him. Maybe even draw the man into him by sheer force of will.

"Slow down, baby. You're even smaller on the inside than you are on the outside. But I can fix that."

The finger stopped but didn't move away. Nicholas heard the snap of another lid and wetness oozed down his crack to his opening, leaving a path of surprising heat to mark its trail.

His ass clenched, bearing down on the unexpected invasion of the entire tip of Erp's finger. It spasmed, instantly rebelling against the intrusion. Yet Nicholas felt a stirring of excitement in the pit of his stomach. He concentrated on relaxing, breathing slowly through his mouth and pushing down, encouraging Erp to go deeper.

"Oh, yeah. Damn, you're so small. Let's do this right." More gel was slathered between his ass cheeks, shocking and cold then teasingly warm. Erp worked the gel into the tight ring, the heat relaxing the muscles but intensifying the pleasant burn of being coaxed open.

The finger reached deeper, stroking his insides, turning and exploring as if Erp was looking to snag the brass ring on an old-fashioned merry-go-round. Nicholas grunted and squirmed. He was embarrassed by his body's position but thrilled by the way Erp's free hand continued to rub his back and sides, almost a cherishing caress that helped dissolve some of the first time tension away.

Then Erp touched a spot and tension snapped through Nicholas like a burst of thunder. His ears buzzed, his skin flushed, and fine hairs all over his body stood up. Even his fingertips tingled. His cock expanded, swollen too large for its skin, his racing heartbeat pulsing in the arteries deep under the flesh of his stiff cock. Pre-cum coated the head, painting a trail of passion on his belly. He spread his knees to allow his dick to rub on the bedspread, delighting in the friction of the nubby texture.

His opening spread and the finger sunk deeper, a firm, smooth in and out stroke that managed to touch parts of Nicholas he didn't even realize possessed the ability to give him pleasure. Erp probed and rubbed, adding a circling motion to the rhythm, coaxing the muscles wider with each sensual inch of entrance gained.

Nicholas concentrated on the new sensations Erp was awakening, battling to keep his orgasm from building too quickly while savoring the multiple waves of lust and need rushing to encompass his every fiber.

Suddenly Erp's body heat was everywhere. The big man leaned close and wrapped his free arm around Nicholas's waist. Nicholas wanted it to wrap around his cock, but Erp seemed to be avoiding that part of his body.

His flesh was scalding against Nicholas's, breathtaking in intensity. The scent of earthy sweat was in Nicholas's nostrils, mixed with the aroma of sex and lotion.

Something wet and rough touched him, licking and mouthing the soft spot where neck met shoulder, the unexpected thrill of it forcing a shudder down his bowed spine. His gaze fell on the dark, damp handprint by his face. Nicholas imagined one of those massive, stout fingers in the wet outline deep inside of him. He didn't try to stop the groan or the automatic thrust of his hips backward. He wanted more, needed more.

He wiggled his ass, thrusting in time to the pumping strokes, pulling a panted grunt from his partner. The stroking of his channel became a deep thrust and twist, each powerful pass brushing over the electric charged nub.

"I'm ready. Do it. Please, just do it!"

"'Kay. We'll start this way. It'll be easier for you. Once you're relaxed, we'll make it more personal. Promise."

Erp's flat palm slapped his ass cheek, a deliberate spanking action. Nicholas could feel the handprint on his ass, a tingling burn that contrasted with the pleasurable burn at his stretched asshole. The same, but different, painful but not.

"This is… good. S-seriously. Good."

"Better is coming up soon, baby." Erp eased off Nicholas's back. Nicholas gasped, then froze, his ass clenching and unclenching, grabbing at nothing, suddenly devoid of stimulus and wanting. He wanted to cry out, beg to be rescued from the emptiness that made his belly ache to be filled again. The faint sound of foil being torn then slick pressure pushed at his opening. His asshole fluttered and blossomed, spreading wide to accept its newest invader.

Nicholas had expected Erp to step up his preparation to using two fingers, but as the ring of muscle at his opening popped around a solid, hot cylinder of flesh he realized he was riding Erp's thick, veined dick. He shivered with the knowledge, breath lost to the slow battering thrust of iron cock sliding into this body.

Erp pumped and heaved, his breathing short pants, sweat dripping off him to splash on Nicholas's skin. His hands drew Nicholas's hips up and back with each thrust, his thumbs holding Nicholas's cheeks apart, forcing the tiny hole wider, letting his cock sink into Nicholas until he was balls deep.

"Shit! Now!" The familiar fizzy buzz began to build in the pit of Nicholas's lower abdomen, his balls going tight, his head swimming in overload. All of it happening too fast for him to savor the moment.

"Not yet."

Pressure clamped at the base of his cock and a sharp slap to the head of his dick broke off the escalating climb toward eruption. Tears sprung to his eyes. He choked on them as he swallowed them down, soothed slightly by firm massaging of fingertips over his abused dick.

"Sorry, but I'd like to see you when you come." The cock in his ass slid out while the vise-like grip on Nicholas's hips tightened. Powerful hands lifted and flipped him in the air, then gently lowering him to the bed. His bent knees and his legs fell to the sides. He instinctively wrapped them around Erp's waist.

Erp's cock rose up between Nicholas's thighs, shining wet, a dark bronze, condom-capped pole of roped veins and dripping clear gel streaked with swirls of creamy white. He was panting, his broad chest heaving, glistening in the sunlight, his skin covered in sweat, groin and hands smeared with lube. He towered over Nicholas. The victorious Viking warrior that legends were written about.

Erp wasted no time guiding his rigid dick back up Nicholas's eager hole. Nicholas gasped at the sensation of being filled, the sudden stretch and burn renewed, the slap of flesh against flesh, the smell of sex and desire, the slick, velvet thrust of cock all made his senses reel.

"Grab my neck. Want you close." Erp tugged, lifted, and instantly Nicholas was hanging in the air, his back floating over the bed, his heels digging into Erp's solid, bare ass, his cock rubbing over the rigid six-pack of the man's rippled abdomen. "I like my lovers small for a reason. Just like you like them big."

Hands grabbed under his ass. Erp lifted Nicholas's body and pulled him down on his shaft as he arched his back and thrust up. They bodies slammed together, burying Erp deeper than before. Deep enough he nudged Nicholas's sweet spot with each inward stroke. Erp's weighty balls spanked Nicholas's ass and the crisp hair of his groin grated over the sensitive, exposed areas of his perineum. It was heaven.

Nicholas swung in mid-air supported by the sheer strength of his partner's beefy arms. Power flowed around and through him, as if his body was plugged into a sexually charged powerhouse battery instead of a man. This, this feeling of strength, domination, and an exhilarating sense of helplessness was what he loved, what he could only find with a gentle giant of a lover. Erp was everything Nicholas dreamed about, everything his body ached for, everything his mind looked for in a partner. Two hundred and eighty pounds of pure nirvana on two legs with a cock as thick as Nicholas' wrist.

The jarring thrusts grew more urgent. Nicolas swore he could feel Erp's cock still growing inside of him.

Just as he was seriously thinking of freeing one hand to work his own dick in time to the rapid rhythm, Erp slowed and dropped to his knees, taking Nicholas with him. The bed's low platform matched Erp's hip height exactly. Nicholas landed on his back, his ass hanging over the edge of the mattress, still riding Erp's thick, pounding shaft.

Gripping his thighs, Erp yanked him closer. A palm as rough as fine sandpaper engulfed his cock and the world spun away, leaving Nicholas on fire. He groaned, panted, the sensations too good to be real, too real to want to ever stop, too mind blowing to continue for much longer.

And just when he didn't think it could get any better, one of those same sandpaper coarse palms caressed his cheek and jaw, titling his face to allow their mouths to seal together. The kiss was all wet tongue, soft lips and breathy moans. Scorching. Mind melting, erotic beyond belief.

Who said real men don't kiss?

His stomach knotted. His lungs felt paralyzed. A violent tremor seized him and his skin turned to molten heat. His ass clenched with a powerful squeeze that felt as if it could crush the stout cock buried inside him. A spasm raced along the length of the bruising intruder.

Nicholas felt every velvety ridge, every poker stiff inch of Erp's cock. He imagined the head hitting the sweet spot deep inside in his ass, rubbing, dragging its smooth, cream-slicked cap over the tiny nub, almost like a tongue licking its spongy surface. The opening to his asshole was a ring of fire, the muscles stretched wider than they had ever been before, tightly, desperately hugging the hefty circumference of Erp's battering dick.

The burn was painful at first, a fiery discomfort that almost instantly morphed into a sizzling pleasure. The intensity of the burn grew with each new stroke into his channel, the sensation spread inward, crawling up his ass like a network of newly awakened nerve endings experiencing life for the first time.

The slick slap of wet flesh echoed in his head, dirty and forbidden. It was an audible rhythm of thrust and withdraw, erotic background music for his own nearly constant moans.

The heaviness of Erp's solid hands gripping him was arousing on their own. They held him tight, manhandling his slender body wherever Erp wanted it, dominating, controlling his every action. He was totally at the big man's mercy, a prisoner in his brawny, cradling arms. Even his lips and tongue had surrendered to the man, allowing his mouth to be ravaged, his very breath consumed.

Nicholas had never been more aroused, more completely possessed by another lover. Erp invaded his mouth, tasting and marking him, took his body hostage, his flesh staked on the man's plundering cock, each deep invasion of his ass leaving something of the big man inside of him. Fanciful as it was, a part of Nicholas burst open and a rush of emotion flowed through him, making his chest ache.

He felt his orgasm begin to teeter on the edge of explosion. All he needed was one tiny shove and he would fall off the cliff into blissful sexual oblivion. He yearned for one harsh stroke of his cock, one deeper thrust into his body, or one more delicious lap of tongue over tongue to set him off, but the final igniting act was less blatant.

Erp settled his weight down on Nicholas, lying chest to chest, a living blanket of warm, sweat-coated flesh engulfed not just his body but his consciousness as well. Erp wrapped an arm under Nicholas's hips to help support their position, making sure their rhythm wasn't lost.

His other hand caressed the side of Nicholas's face, a gentle cherishing touch that shook Nicholas to the core. Then Erp kissed him, a scorching, ravenous kiss that claimed every inch of Nicholas's mouth. A hand wove through his damp hair and tugged, a sharp biting pain that notched his excitement higher and he opened his lips wider, desperate for more.

A shudder ran from his scalp to his cock, and out the tips of his toes. He beat his heels against Erp's clenched ass, curling his hips up into the thrusts, sinking Erp's cock impossibly deeper. He could feel every inch of the shaft, his channel clinging to it, his opening so tight around the thick base he imagined he could sense Erp's hammering pulse through it. Fresh waves of heat rippled along his dangling nerves. His long denied orgasm burst to life, fireworks dimming his vision and sapping his strength.

Erp sucked harder on Nicholas's tongue and each gulp triggered another violent spasm in his channel. Nicholas groaned and thrashed. Wave after wave of powerful contractions exploded in his lower belly.

Cum spurted from his dick in short creamy ropes, each eruption so gloriously thrilling it was next to painful in the pleasure it gave him. It oiled their skin, bathing their abdomens, adding a sensuously dirty, wet noise to their coupling.

A tight knot contorted his gut. His balls ached with the effort to proclaim his orgasm. The skin on his dick felt two sizes too small for his still swollen shaft. Empty of cum, it continued to pulse and quiver, dry shooting long after his juices were spent. His chest strained with each panted breath, sucking in air around Erp's insistent kiss, his skin covered in gooseflesh. His limbs quaking with relief, his body reluctant to surrender to the last pulses of orgasm. Nicholas wanted this glorious feeling of being captured and claimed to go on forever.

Exhausted, Nicholas's arms fell away from Erp's shoulders. His legs dropped limply to the bed, his thighs still spread wide around Erp's still pumping hips.

Suddenly Erp broke the kiss, his head arching up, his back ramrod stiff. He shuddered and froze, cock buried deep, his powerful square fingers yanking Nicholas harder onto his dick, their imprint making the skin of Nicholas's hips white against their golden tan. Warmth flooded his ass, seeping into the hidden passage of his body. He knew Erp was wearing a condom but he imagined his insides coated with Erp's cum, staining his flesh with the man's essence. Nicholas could smell it in the air, feel its wetness tickle out his opening between rapid frantic thrusts.

Collapsing, Erp tucked Nicholas close, literally curling around him. Nicholas caught a glimpse of Erp's expression before he buried into the crook of Nicholas's neck, the strong, chiseled face beautifully twisted in the rapture of climax. A strained grunt of pure satisfaction rumbled in his throat, followed by a groan so primal and sexy Nicholas's ass clenched at the mere sound of it.

Time slowed down. Nicholas lost himself in the afterglow of climax, vaguely registering loss of Erp's dick as it slid out of his body, the fresh wave of protest from his asshole, the final surrender of his own cock as it folded limply to one side, shriveled and spent. Then his body was tugged up over grainy, damp sheets, the swift, casual action more a superhero's move than that of an ordinary lover.

From under drowsy lids, Nicholas watched Erp roll to his back, stretching out so far his massive arms and legs touched both ends of the bed. Then he rolled on his side to face Nicholas, a smile on his chapped lips and a tender look in his eyes. He ran a sticky hand over Nicholas's abdomen and chest. "You were fantastic."

"And you're fucking amazing. Perfect." He promised himself he wasn't going to ask. No strings, just casual sex. But it slipped out. "Can we do this again? Sometime soon?"

"Sure." Erp leaned closer giving Nicholas a slow, lingering exploration of lips filled with appreciation and pleasure. It was like a wordless, physical 'thank you.' "Everything about you hits all my hot buttons, Nicky."

Sweat, lotion and cum trickled off their bodies onto the bed, smearing the wrinkled covers. Exhausted, his asshole fluttering, vainly searching for Erp's cock, the tiny spasms reawakened the delicious burn of penetration. He smelled of sex and pleasure he linked directly to Erp. It was heady and satisfying. His first time couldn't have been any better. The thought made his cock jerk with anticipation. Nicholas realized he lay in a puddle of twisted linen, his skin beginning to stick to the dark streaked mass of damp sheets.

Wet sheets.

Now he knew where Erp's private kink came from. It was oddly thrilling to be sated, slick-skinned and surrounded by the results of their sexual playing. Their climax was gone but the physical evidence of their pleasure and emotional connection lay in those sheets.

Dazed, Nicholas blurted out his thoughts. "This was exactly how I'd hoped my first time would be."

"*First time?*" Nicholas found himself scooped up off the bed and dropped on Erp's broad chest. A long leg wound around his legs while large hands with a very solid grip held him in place by his forearms. His cock squirmed in protest at being crushed between them.

"Ah, well…" He swallowed hard and stared into Erp's face, the dark cloud in the man's eyes sent a stab of guilt to his gut. "Not my *first time* first time." He stuttered, trying to remove the look of mistrust from Erp's handsome face. "I've *had* sex before. Sure. Yeah. I mean, *really.*" The cheeks on his face burned as much as his ass did.

"What *did* you mean then, Nicky?" The grip on his arms tightened slightly then relaxed quickly, as if Erp suddenly realized how strong of a hold he had on them.

"Ah. First time… with a guy twice my size?" Erp barely flexed his biceps and Nicholas's entire body traveled over Erp's torso until they were eye to eye. He never had been a good liar.

"I don't think so." Then understanding seemed to dawn on Erp, his expression going from distrustful to horrified. "You weren't nervous about me snapping you in two earlier."

Okay, horror mixed with no little bit of anger.

"You were worried I'd *split* you in two. You've never done this before have you?"

Vibrations radiated through Erp's body into Nicholas's. He could literally feel the big man straining to keep from shaking him until his teeth rattled. Nicholas blushed, blinking to keep up the courage required to continue meeting Erp's accusing stare.

"Yes. Well, no. This was my first time, you know… taking it." Erp's unhappy expression didn't waver. His lips were still set in disapproving thin line. His hold on Nicholas tightened slightly, preventing Nicholas's casual attempt to slip off Erp's body and escape the gathering storm cloud. Nicholas gave in to the inevitable and settled back into place. "But you were great!"

"You should have told me. I could have hurt you, you little idiot!"

"No! You took good care of me, Erp." He grabbed Erp's solid shoulders and dug his fingers in, revealing a little of his own wiry strength. He wasn't a weakling, he just had a kink for being manhandled by a larger lover. A much larger lover.

"I'm fine. *More than fine.* It was *fucking fabulous.*" Nicholas locked gazes with Erp, relieved as the anger etched around the man's expressive eyes and mobile lips muted into exasperation then grudging acceptance of the facts. "I think part of that *fabulous* was because it was you inside of me. You're awesome, he-man."

A snort of laughter broke the tension. Nicholas joined in with a wary chuckle. Erp smiled, shaking his head. His restraining grip turned into a comforting embrace as he wrapped his arms around Nicholas's back, crushing them together chest to chest.

"Next time, I'll show you what rimming is like. That'll relax that sweet little virgin ass of yours like nothing else."

"There's going to be a next time?"

"Tight little asses need lots of lube and lotion." Erp hands slid down Nicholas's sweaty back and groped the slippery crack of his ass before pressing a long finger into him. It slid in easily, making a hungry, slurping sound when Erp wiggled the digit. Nicholas's cock instantly came alive, struggling to full erection between their bodies. "That is if you can get used to lying in wet sheets."

"Must be the Viking in you looking for the sea. Bring it on, he-man."

THE CATARACTS

PART TWO

WILLIAM MALTESE

Kyle is surprised. I see that as soon as I'm out of Cary Blight's enfolding strong arms with another laugh in appreciation of delightful reunion.

I'm a little embarrassed. My rush down the stairs and into Cary's firm embrace was reminiscent of long-lost friends (lovers?) rather than two people whose acquaintance consists of a few hours on a plane ride between Rio and Iguassu.

"How very, very good to see you, again," I tell Cary. How quickly I've broken my agreement with Kyle to stay in my room while he entertains business associates.

"Imagine my surprise," Cary says and sounds pleased. "I hoped I might see you as soon as I found I was coming here."

"Are you staying long?"

Cary gives a questioning look to the woman with him; her expression is curious amusement.

It had been the female voice which pulled my attention to the trio in the first place. I assume she's Maria Malendez.

She's tall, beautiful, and svelte. She has high cheekbones, accentuated by her brown hair pulled back severely to form small chignon in the nape of her impressively long neck. Her eyes are large and brown, child-like behind long fan-length lashes. Her eyes stay focused on me, but she speaks in response to Cary's unvoiced question.

"It's up to Kyle, really," Maria said. At the last minute, she shifts her gaze to Kyle, arching her left eyebrow by way of some unasked question of her own.

"I'm sure you and Mr. Blight will have time to talk over old times a little later on, William," Kyle says. "Now, if you'll excuse us, please?"

I'm more than a little piqued by his dismissive tone. If he's miffed by my butting in, how could I have known Cary was one of his expected business associates?

"Later then, William," Cary promises and turns to follow Kyle and Maria across the room and into the door-soon-closed-behind-them library.

I return to my room and to the lunch Pedro has brought on the pushcart. I leave my door open to catch any sounds of Kyle, Maria, and/or Cary emerging from their downstairs conference.

What business, I wonder, can Cary have with Kyle? As I literally destroy a piece of so-English cold toast with a so-English cold pat of butter, I try to remember anything Cary said about his job during our plane flight in. It had all been about mining.

I'm brought from my reverie by a noise at my open door. I look up to see Jenny Salinas. She looks exceptionally attractive, dressed in a lacy pink pinafore and black patent-leather shoes. Her long black hair is parted in the middle and attractively hangs each side of her face.

She fidgets, obviously ill at ease. If she's there to see me, she doesn't look directly at me. She looks at her feet, shifting them nervously, from side to side, on the floor.

"Jenny?" I wipe my hands free of crumbled toast. "Can I do something for you, honey?"

She turns, I think it's to leave. Instead, she stays and pulls the door shut behind her. She walks across the floor and stops a few feet away. With apparently great effort, she lifts her head.

"I've come to apologize for screaming at you," she says.

"I accept your apology." I have very little experience with children. I suspect we have little in common. "I understand from your uncle that the two of you are especially fond of this place."

She doesn't answer. Her head droops again, and she goes back to shifting her weight from foot to foot.

"Your Uncle Kyle tells me you were born here," I try again. "Don't you miss not having any other children your age to play with?"

"No!" She's emphatic. Her head comes up and her eyes tear in emphasis.

"Really, honey," I provide a helpless little laugh, "I'm really just trying to make conversation. I'm not used to little girls, or to little boys. I've never had brothers or sisters, nieces or nephews…"

She provides me with a look of momentarily repentance; her right hand shifts a few stray hair strands out of her eyes.

"Why don't you sit in that chair?" I nod in the indicated direction. "I'm sure we can find something to talk about."

She shuffles nervously and gives a quick look back toward the door. She reminds me of some small and very vulnerable little animal about to be caught in the jaws of some very large predator. However, she accepts my invitation and moves to the chair and sits. She folds her hands in her lap and looks at them.

"How about school?" I'm willing to let the rest of my meal go cold to see what's up with this little girl.

"It's summer vacation," she says. "I have a tutor, she's on holiday."

"Do you like your tutor?" I try to put across genuine interest that I'm not feeling.

"She's okay … I guess." Once again, her eyes are on the closed door.

"Do you see a lot of *Senora* and *Senor* Malendez?" I hope my question sounds innocent.

"Her husband is dead," she says in a very low voice.

"Are she and your uncle very close?"

Jenny doesn't seem any more relaxed than when she first appeared, but I'm still out to make myself more informed as to my previous suspicions regarding her Uncle Kyle. Although Kyle and Maria strike me as an attractive couple, I don't ask Jenny if, by chance, her uncle is bisexual.

"Maria and Uncle Kyle grew up together," the girl says, swinging one leg and then the other beneath her chair.

"She's a neighbor?"

Jenny nods in such a way that references any direction within three-hundred-and-sixty degree.

"She runs her place by herself now that her husband is dead, does she?" I continue my detective work.

"She has hired help." Jenny examines the small ball her fingers make in her lap.

"Your uncle sometimes gives her a hand..." *More likely his hard dick* "...does he?" I'm trying not to wonder why I find it so important to define the Kyle-Maria relationship.

"Sometimes, yes." So, she is prepared to be more specific if prodded. I'm encouraged. "Uncle Kyle says Maria is more capable than her husband ever was."

"Capable and beautiful into the bargain." I say more to myself than to Jenny.

"You think she's beautiful?" The young girl's eyes, dark brown, make contact with mine.

"Yes, of course," I say. "Don't you?"

"Oh, sure," Jenny says. "I've always thought so.

"You find it surprising, though, that I do?"

"I asked Uncle Kyle once if he thought Maria was beautiful. He took a very long time before finally saying yes."

I wait, sure she'll go on. She doesn't do anything but drop her gaze back to her lap where she's folding and unfolding her fingers.

"Then, I guess we all agree, at least on that one thing," I conclude.

Jenny looks up and surprises me with, "Do you think you're handsome, then?"

I'm at a momentary loss.

"Beauty and handsomeness are always in the eye of the beholder, honey," I risk being hopelessly trite.

"Uncle Kyle says you're exceptionally good-looking," Jenny says, her eyes back on the closed door. "I didn't even have to ask him. He said it on his own. 'There, Jenny, is one very good-looking man, and he knows it, too.' That's what he said."

Don't ask why I'm blushing. I haven't a clue. I do admit to being strangely pleased by this second-hand compliment. Simultaneously, I wonder how Maria Malendez would react to Kyle having made such a statement about a man. And if Maria could accept any such statement, without experiencing any jealousy, what would she say and do if she knew Kyle had kissed me? Or, maybe, she's willing to overlook whatever Kyle might think he has to do to keep control of *The Cataracts*. His dalliances with me simply expedience, and not because of any real same-sex sexual ardor.

"*I* think you're handsome, too," Jenny says. "I like your blond hair."

"Why, thank you, honey; I think you're beautiful, too."

"My mother was blonde." She has ignored my compliment; perhaps she merely accepts it as her due.

"Do you miss your mother?" I can't help wondering what Jeremy's wife had been like.

"I didn't really know her," Jenny says. "She died when I was born. Sometimes, though, I look at pictures my father has of her and him in Rome. Have you ever been?"

"I was in Italy just last year. Rome is a beautiful city. You should go see it yourself sometime."

"That's what daddy says." She sits straighter; her voice has taken on a harsher tone.

"Your father just gets lonesome for the places and people he remembers before he came here, Jenny," I say.

Her response is an accusatory stare.

Someone has to set this little girl straight — Jeremy shouldn't be made to play the heavy in the eyes of his own daughter — and that someone might as well be me.

"You're upset, because your father wants to take you away from here. It disturbs you, because this is the place you know best. These are surroundings in which you feel most comfortable. On the other hand, your daddy feels more at home in Rome, and Paris, and London. There are some unhappy things he remembers here."

"Like grandma, you mean?" Jenny's voice retains its defensiveness.

"Yes, like your grandmother."

"She didn't commit suicide, you know!" Jenny says loudly. "I'll bet that's what father told you happened, didn't he?" She doesn't wait for me to deny or confirm. She gets to her feet, her face contorted and no longer very pretty. "Grandma got drunk and fell."

She runs to the door but pulls back at the last minute, as if she's been delivered a sizable electric jolt. She stands, trembling, her back toward me.

I'd like to provide some sort of consolation, but I haven't a clue. I refuse to cheer her up by running her father down.

She audibly starts to sob.

"Whether your grandmother was drunk, or whether she committed suicide, really doesn't make all that much difference in the long run, don't you agree, Jenny?" I squat beside her. "The fact remains that your father's mother did fall and did die as a result. Whatever the reason, living with that having happened so close by can hardly be all that easy for your father."

"He hates it here," she says. "He hates Uncle Kyle. He hates me."

"Oh, Jenny, honey, I really do doubt that your father hates you even one bit."

"He does!" She turns on me with large eyes converted into deep pools of overflowing wet, her cheeks streak with her tears.

"Listen, honey." I put a consoling hand on her shoulder and leave it there only because she doesn't try to shake it free. "It just might sometimes seem that way. After all, it's not an easy thing for a man to raise a child on his own. It's especially hard when the father hasn't been an adult all that long himself. After all, how old is your father? Twenty-five? Twenty-six? And, how old are you? About six?"

"Seven," she says. She sniffs and then wipes her nose on the back of one hand.

"That would only make your father around eighteen when you were born. That's pretty young, Jenny. Being a father is pretty daunting even at an older age."

My mental arithmetic makes me wonder why Jeremy married so early.

"He *does* hate me," Jenny insists, despite all of my efforts. "He really *really* does."

"Let's go find and ask him, shall we?" I reach for the doorknob.

"No!" she says at the exact moment I realize the door is locked from the outside.

I can't believe it and try the door again. Yes, locked! Obviously, the deed was done while I've talked with Jenny. Who closed the door, my having initially left it open? Jenny closed it. Surely, though, Kyle hasn't used the little girl, has he? Nonetheless, there's no doubt in my mind who ordered the key turned and the lock engaged.

I'm surprised at how calm I am. It would be very easy to rant and rave. Maybe I'm just restrained because Jenny is obviously so upset.

"Come on, Jenny, there's no need to cry. Sooner or later someone will come and unlock the door. Until then, the best thing for us to do is sit back and try to make the best of our situation."

It's two hours before Kyle unlocks the door.

"Why don't you go play, now, Jenny?" I say. "Your Uncle Kyle and I have things we need say to each other."

She looks to her uncle for permission. He nods and she leaves the room.

"How nice of you to come to our rescue," I say as soon as Jenny has exited. "It seems Jenny and I were inadvertently locked in."

Kyle doesn't say anything. He stands there, apparently waiting for my next move.

"You may bully your brother all you please," I say, "although I find that bullying an obvious flaw in your character. The minute you start locking me in my room, you've overstepped your boundaries."

"You think so?"

"I *know* so."

"You were surprised by it, then?"

"Of course, I was bloody surprised."

"It had to be obvious that I couldn't allow you in on any private talk with Cary Blight," Kyle says. "Right now, he's very important to me, and I can't afford you turning him against me."

"Which you're sure I would do?" My voice is on the rise despite my on-going effort to keep calm, cool, and collected.

"There was never any question," Kyle says simply. "I saw by your greeting that you could soon have had him eating out of your hand — or dining on some more delectable part of your tasty anatomy."

"I barely know him, if the truth be told." My temper is on the rise.

"You two could have fooled me," Kyle said. You were as close to making love, while fully dressed and standing, as any two men I've ever seen."

"What a disgustingly overactive imagination you have!"

"So, how did you say you know Cary Blight?" Kyle asks.

"We had this mad and passionate love affair while sharing adjoining seats and conversation on an airplane."

"Initiating each other into the Mile-High Club?"

"Very funny!"

"He was definitely very sorry about your sudden migraine."

"My migraine? Oh, of course, my *migraine*."

Kyle would have had to come up with some excuse for my not returning as I'd promised. What had Cary thought upon hearing Kyle's flimsy excuse? Whatever, he apparently accepted it. Why not? How could he guess what was going on here?

"Why don't we both sit down and talk?" Kyle suggests, surprising me no end.

I sit on the bed. He sits in a chair. I wait for him to begin.

"My father left me a piece of land just outside of Asuncion," he says. "Cary Blight has been hired to either negate or substantiate preliminary reports that there may be a deposit of copper on the land. If there is copper in any viable amount, I'll possibly be able to match the hotel's offer for your and my brother's shares of *The Cataracts*. That should make everyone happy, except International Hotels, shouldn't it?"

"What does that have to do with locking me in my room?"

He folds his arms defensively across his broad chest. "I don't want you filling Cary's head with tales of my holding my brother captive. Cary needs all of his attention focused on one thing and one thing only."

"Couldn't you have simply explained all of this to me beforehand, just as you're doing now?"

"I could have, and would have, if I'd had pre-warning that you and Cary were close. Since I didn't, until you two were greeting each other, downstairs, like long-parted-but-finally-reunited-lovers, there was little point in telling you something you'd probably get back to Jeremy. It would be cruel to get my half-brother's hopes up prematurely, only to have them dashed when Cary finds no copper on the property in sufficient quantity or quality to extract profitably."

"Cary found nothing there, then?"

"There are promising samples but nothing yet to indicate there would be a reasonable return on the substantial investment that would be necessary for mining it."

"Why tell me this now?"

"You deserve some explanation as to why I kept you and your friend apart. Your lock up was spontaneous and might not have occurred had I had a bit more time to consider my options. Might I suggest that you don't tell Jeremy for the reason mentioned?"

"I'm loath to forgive you for using your niece to distract me from realizing my door was being locked."

"I suppose you wouldn't believe me if I said I didn't know she was with you?"

"That's a question?"

"I sent Pedro with instructions to lock your door. Do you think I'd willingly risk you the opportunity to brainwash Jenny?"

"Brainwash! She obviously idolizes you. I doubt anything I, or anyone else, could say would convince her otherwise."

"You wouldn't want to give me a quick rundown on what you two talked about, would you? Jenny is vulnerable."

Suddenly, he's up, next to me, and his lips, for not the first time, are on a collision course with mine.

Why don't I turn away? I don't know. A few minutes earlier, held captive in this very room, I hated this man with a passion. And, now ... now ... now?

His lips are as firmly demanding as I remember. His breath tastes of mint. His face smells of exotic after-shave that compliments the lemony scent of his cologne.

"There now, William," Kyle says, finally breaking the kiss. "Why have we wasted so much time fighting each other? You and I aren't inexperienced novices playing at love, are we? We're two adult males who know exactly what we want at this particular moment in time. Which is each other."

"What you really want is my share of *The Cataracts,* if my memory serves me correctly." It would have been so nice pretending that wasn't continually at the back of my mind each time Kyle touched me - denying it didn't make it any less true.

"Oh, William, William, William," Kyle says softly, shaking his head.

His hand withdraws from my face, briefly brushing my lips as it does so. When, in aftermath, I lick my mouth, in reflexive response, I taste him. My dick goes harder than it already is.

"No matter what you might like to think to the contrary," he says," Jeremy never wanted Jenny born. He wanted a boy to whom my ailing father would have given a far larger percentage of *The Cataracts* — over which Jeremy would have had control — than dear daddy could ever bring himself to give a granddaughter."

CHAPTER SEVEN

I'm already packed when I excuse myself from the dinner table by saying, "I have one of my recurring migraines." Kyle smiles at my sarcasm but says and does nothing to prevent me from leaving for my room.

I'm up early the next morning and quick to shower, sans jack-off and attending man-man fantasies. I check closets and drawers in a final assurance that I'm not leaving anything behind.

I hope to catch Kyle over breakfast but only find Pedro cleaning up. Obviously, he's surprised to see me so early, as ever since my arrival, I've taken my breakfasts in my room.

"Is Mr. Salinas somewhere nearby?" Suddenly figuring Pedro might think I refer to Jeremy, I qualify, "I'd like to talk with Kyle this morning if possible."

"He's in the garden," Pedro says and reaches for another dirty dish.

I bee-line for the garden within which I've enjoyed many strolls since my arrival at *The Cataracts*. The morning temperature already hints at the greater heat soon to be had from an upcoming day. There's a mist suspended in the air, but it will soon disperse by literally rolling into the nearby gorge.

There's light dew on the grass, not yet evaporated; it glosses my shoes. My walking leaves visible footprints in the moisture.

I walk the front of the house, past the banyan. The garden is laid out in precise geometrical design maintained by two gardeners who I've often spied at work.

I don't immediately spot Kyle, but that doesn't mean he isn't there. There are several large hedges that form a labyrinth that can conceal a whole company of people. The maze of shrubbery initially confused me, but I've since realized it's merely a simple series of circular pathways that open, one onto the other, the final and central one opening upon a large fountain.

The fountain is marble and exquisitely baroque, recalling the Rome of my summer the year before. It has four life-size rearing horses, each facing a major compass point. A large shallow bowl is supported by the horses' necks. From the bowl, two nymphs and two satyrs emerge to support a central dolphin whose mouth constantly spews the water that rains the shallow bowl to overflow and fill an even larger, lower, marble surround.

Kyle sits the edge of the latter basin. He glances up, obviously as surprised to see me as Pedro was. His pleasant smile indicates my interruption isn't necessarily unwelcome.

"Good morning, William. Whatever brings you to life this early in the day?"

I sit on the edge of the fountain beside him. The high banks of surrounding hedges mute enough of the distant roar of cataracts so that fountain splashes are the dominant sounds. We can easily hear each other when speaking in our normal voices.

"Have you eaten breakfast?" His hand trails the pool and causes circular eddies, otherwise, the water is crystal clear and readily reveals the intricate seafloor-motif of the mosaic at its bottom.

Kyle's eyes are exceptionally violet in the early morning sunshine. His lashes are so dark and so long. His tanned face is clean-shaven. I can just make out the blue-black shadow that will be his beard should it ever be allowed it to grow. He wears tight-fitting riding pants, calf-high black boots, and a snug polo shirt that's open at its collar to reveal the black hair curling on his exquisitely muscled chest.

"I want to talk." Suddenly, I'm sorry I never got around to strolling the garden after nightfall, the only time its verbena condescends to release heavy sweet fragrance to the air.

"Sounds as if you intend to spoil an absolutely perfect morning." When he smiles, I notice, for not the first time, the sexy dimpling of his right cheek. "Our conversations have the record for being downright disastrous."

"Not this one," I promise.

"All right, then."

"I'd like you to make arrangements, as soon as possible, for someone to drive me to the airport. I've decided to leave you and Jeremy to settle your own differences. I'm going to head on back and try to put my own life in order."

From him, I expect abject joy, sheer delight, overpowering relief, and undying gratitude. I get none of that.

"I thought you'd be jumping in excitement with that news," I admit. "Maybe, you didn't hear me?"

"I heard you." His inflection is neutral.

"I'm not accomplishing anything by staying," I say. "I've only seen Jeremy a few times since my arrival. My whole point for being here was business with him which now sees little hope of ever being accomplished. I'm no longer even sure signing over my percentage of *The Cataracts* to him is the best for all involved, Jeremy included."

"I'm glad you've at least achieved that much insight," he says.

"That said, I remain sympathetic enough to Jeremy's way of thinking not to want to do anything that might betray him, either."

"I shall miss you," he says with such seeming sincerity that I almost believe him.

"I'm sure that you and *Senora* Malendez will manage very well without me."

"Maria having just what to do with what?"

"She's very attractive."

"Yes, and ...?"

"Really, it's none of my business." I wish I'd left the attractive Maria Malendez out of it.

He starts laughing. When he stops, finally, he says, "Maria is like a sister to me. When I needed working capital I didn't have so your handsome friend Blight could check out the copper potential of my property, Maria advanced me enough for the survey."

"As I said, it's none of my business."

"Surely, it's not because of Maria that you've been so stand-offish?"

I wish he'd get me my transportation to the airport. If we're not careful, this conversation is going to disintegrate as have most of our others.

"I do keep getting all of these I'm-available vibrations from you," he says, "but keep getting shot down each and every time I make a pass."

"It never occurred to you that not every man is bowled over by your charm — or lack thereof?"

"What are you afraid of, William?" He slides closer. "Am I such a bad guy to see you so quickly packing? Or, is it just that you continue to think I'm out to seduce you only because of your percentage in *The Cataracts*?"

"What I think, or do not think, I'm no longer planning to sell either you or your half-brother my interest. This, as I see it, leaves me little reason to remain."

"Well, let me show you what *I* intend to do before you run, shall I?"

He takes me in his large muscular arms and pulls me toward him. His lips land firmly on my mouth. I feel the solid definition of his chest, while the more intimate muscle tautness of his one thigh hard-presses against me.

He breaks the kiss, and touches his lips gently to each of my reflexively closed eyelids, to my cheeks, to my neck.

My face goes hot from what's happening. My heart beats louder with each additional second I'm kissed in his arms.

What this all boils down to is very simple. Do I want this to end — whatever *this* is —or do I want this to continue? Should I deprive myself of what I'm more and more convinced I want — only because the man I want it with and from has motives probably less motivated by genuine affection than I would like them to be, especially my first time around?

My decision is made for me by Kyle pushing me away and gazing intently over my shoulder to …

Pedro stands breathless on the sidelines. For how long has he been there, and what all has he seen?

Pedro says something rapidly in Spanish about Jeremy, about Jenny.

Kyle turns pale. Whatever Pedro's obviously bad news, he heads on back the way he came in.

"Well, haven't I been the royal fool?" Kyle says, his eyes gone smoky and filled with accusatory sparks.

"What?" As usual, I haven't a clue.

"How clever that innocent little façade of yours, William," he accuses. "Unfortunately for you and your travel plans, we've discovered Jeremy and Jenny are gone before you can join them."

CHAPTER EIGHT

A balcony surrounds most of the house wing in the banyan. There's usually sunshine on some part of that balcony at all times of any day. There are lounge chairs. There are small tables upon which to put cool drinks or snacks scrounged from the kitchen.

I take advantage of this cloudless day. Wearing the skimpy European-cut swimsuit I picked up in physique-flaunting Rio, and bringing along a book borrowed from *The Cataracts'* library, I stake out my claim in the embracing sunshine.

When Kyle pulls up in front of the house, driving the Jeep (I wasn't even aware he'd gone out), I purposely pay no attention to his wave. It has been two days since Jeremy and Jenny disappeared.

Kyle insists that it will only be a matter of time before he's tracked them down and brought them back. According to Kyle, Jeremy doesn't have enough cash to last anywhere for very long, not the way he likes to spend it. Without me on the outside with him to sign papers, there's not much chance he'll replenish whatever his dwindling finances, either.

Kyle is convinced Jenny unlocked her father's door. He's also convinced that the whole incident was spawned within those couple of hours I spent locked-up alone with the girl. Kyle has congratulated me on my skills at playing my part in the conspiracy. He says I'm hypocritical to have chided him for using the child only to turn around and use her myself.

There's no point in trying to explain, one more time, that if Jenny unlocked her father's door, and ran off with him, I had no conscious part in it. Granted, I spent a good amount of time trying to explain to Jenny her father's possible outlook on certain things — a side which had obviously been neglected up until then.

"I thought maybe you could use someone to give you a hand in putting lotion on your back," Kyle says, stepping out on the balcony to join me.

"No, thanks." I turn another page of my book, even though I haven't finished reading it.

"I've decided not to hold any grudges," he says. He selects an adjoining lounge chair and sits down. He's changed his shirt somewhere en route from the Jeep. He was wearing a white pullover, he now wears a short-sleeve gray shirt with its two top two buttons unfastened.

Nonchalantly, I flip another page, having completely lost any thread of the book's plot.

"Is Harold Kline your boyfriend, or something?" He surprises the hell out of me.

"Harold?" How is it possible I've forgotten all about Harold?

"I don't know why, but you never gave me the impression of someone with an official boyfriend waiting in the wings."

"Harold called?"

"He's done better than call, he's here. Well, not here, *here*, but in Iguassu."

"You're kidding!"

"He's worried that you've been carried off by indigenous head hunters with ill intent."

Harold definitely hadn't arrived at *The Cataracts* in the Jeep with Kyle.

"We have him at Maria's until we can think what to do with him." Kyle solves the mystery and locks his fingers behind his head. He eyes me curiously. "We've told him you're off in the jungle on a little field trip and won't be back for a couple days. Hopefully by that time, we'll have located Jeremy and Jenny, then, you and Harold can go off together and do whatever it is boyfriends do."

He stretches sensuously, pointing his toes. His eyes haven't left mine.

"You certainly have a bevy of hot and horny men panting after you, don't you, William? My half-brother. Cary Blight. Me. Now, this boyfriend out of the blue."

The sun seems exceptionally hot.

"You don't kiss like you have a boyfriend." Kyle's voice drips amusement.

I reach for my robe and get up, none too gracefully.

Kyle gets up, his movement as fluid and as graceful as a cat.

"Harold really isn't your type," he says.

"What would you know about my type?" I don't mind my harboring such thoughts about Harold's inadequacies, but I don't want Kyle putting any thoughts into words. Harold, after all, is a marvelous man, come all of this way to find me. Kyle, acutely lacking in the kind-and-considerate department, could gain from Harold's example.

"Apparently, I know more about your type than you do — if you think for one minute you can ever be happy with that guy."

I take a few steps forward in the hopes that Kyle will reflexively step to one side to let me by. He doesn't budge.

He reaches for and snatches my robe from me, giving it an unceremonious toss into the chair he's just vacated. He grabs and yanks me up against him, hard, kissing me so quickly that I'm not even sure what's happening until it's over and done.

I'm furious to see the *gotcha*-twinkle of amusement sparkling his purple eyes.

"You're too much man for Harold or my half-brother," he says.

I break from him - more likely, he lets me go.

I leave my robe behind and force the glass door open along its metal runner.

"Quit kidding yourself *and* poor Harold, William!" Kyle's voice follows after me.

Just who does Kyle think he is that he somehow thinks he has the right to dominate his half-brother's life, his niece's life, and now mine?

I go to my room and take a cold shower, which doesn't take care of the boner that Kyle's kiss, and memory thereof, has caused. I refuse to beat my meat soft or let the spray do it for me.

By the time I've patted dry with a very large Turkish towel, I feel better but only slightly less horny.

I consider not going down for lunch, but I'm hungry. I've been eating like a horse since I've checked in here. That has to stop — but not today.

"There you are," Kyle greets me at the bottom of the stairs. "All ready to go?"

"Go where?" I'm hoping it's to see Harold, but Kyle's mischievous little-boy look tells me that's not likely.

"On a picnic, of course. Everything is packed and ready to go."

"Since when?"

"I know a great spot."

"Get serious!"

The man is impossible.

"Still so much for you to see," he says. "You'll be leaving us before long; if you don't see it now, you likely never see it."

I remind myself that I was furious with him but minutes before. I even remember why. So, where is my anger now? How dangerously and easily he manipulates my emotions.

Certainly, though, he's right. I'm not long destined for this place. Soon, I'll be back in London, all of this behind me. So …

Reluctantly, I end up, once again, in the Jeep with Kyle. He takes the circular driveway toward the jungle and the road that leads toward the airport.

Having not left *The Cataracts* since my arrival, I try to recognize familiar landmarks from my ride in. I recognize nothing. It would take a botanist to differentiate one stretch of this jungle greenery from another.

"Hold on!" Kyle yells above the hot blasting wind that engulfs us as he turns the Jeep off the road and into the underbrush.

"Jesus!" My response as the Jeep enters a small depression and exits, airborne, to land with a jolt.

Kyle steers a zigzag course through trees and bushes. We rock back and forth as the Jeep swerves left and right.

Twice we barrel across small streams and spread fan-like wedges of displaced water.

It's as if we're on some wild amusement-park ride. On more than one occasion, I think we're destined for a head-on with a tree. On each occasion, Kyle maneuvers us to safety.

Suddenly, we're out of the thick jungle and speeding through open meadow filled with pink and blue flowers supported by equally tall and spiky stalks. We leave a heavy aroma of bruised blossoms and scattered petals in our wake.

The Jeep picks up speed; masochistically, I don't want it to stop. There's an exhilarating thrill to moving through this primitive landscape that's surrounded on three sides by equally primitive lush green jungle and suddenly up-thrust crags of blue-green stone.

The Jeep shoots right, almost in a return to the jungle, then left.

Ahead, several birds take wing, fleeing destruction beneath Jeep wheels. I'm fascinated by how we overtake them. For an instant, I can reach out and almost touch one's brightly colored plumage.

The meadow ends, the Jeep bumps over several large rocks and commences another zigzag pattern. This time, instead of avoiding trees, we're hard-pressed to avoid large-and-getting-larger boulders. The Jeep moves onto an upgrade, the steepness of which presses me firmly back in my seat like an astronaut launched into outer space.

Kyle brakes in a small gravel-filled gully. A shroud of dust, until then behind us, catches up. Kyle, his face flushed, laughs. I cough.

In the rearview mirror, I appear dipped in ash.

"Lovely place for a picnic," I sarcastically manage finally. All the greenery has been left behind us. We're in a small cul-de-sac of bare rocks. Dusty stones climb all sides, except to our rear. The Jeep has just enough room in which to turn around, although Kyle makes no effort to make the vehicle do so.

"A small bit of hiking is now in order, that's all," Kyle says. He climbs out of the Jeep. He reaches into the back and hoists a large wicker picnic basket. "This way."

There's a rough stairway etched into an incline. Up he goes. Up I follow.

A seemingly hot and dust-clogged eternity later, we emerge, sweaty, upon a wide table of rock whose far edge drops before us to the valley far below. Miles and miles of lush green jungle, velvety in its interaction with light and shadow, stretches to distant trees fogged by the roil of the cataracts.

"Well," Kyle says, smiling, "was it worth the effort, or what?"

It's a perfect eagle's-nest panorama. The breeze that washes up and over the lip of the cliff is pleasantly cool.

I see no signs of civilization at any of the compass points. It's as if Kyle and I are suddenly the only two people in this entire green world of rock and jungle vegetation.

He puts down the picnic basket and begins unpacking it. First out is a red-and-white checkered tablecloth whose corners he anchors with loose stones.

"Are we expecting a harvest crew to join us?" I ask after he's conjured fried chicken, potato and macaroni salads, yellow and orange and white cheeses, pitted large black olives…

"We're growing boys," he excuses.

A bottle of House Draqual Cabernet Sauvignon 2005BV materializes, and Kyle inserts a screw into its cork.

Our wine glasses are the same Baccarat we used the night we dined in the tree house. I'm surprised they've survived the jarring ride in.

"To fond memories of boyfriends past," he says lifting his glass in toast.

"How about we skip that one and both promise not to mention Harold or Jeremy or Jenny or Maria?" I suggest. "Do you think we can manage that for a couple of hours?"

"Don't know," Kyle says, seemingly in deep thought. "Might be bit hard. Speaking of hard..." His free hand drops to his crotch. There's little imagination needed to see what's not hidden all that well by his pants.

I take a large swallow of the red wine in my glass and wonder if I've ever seen any man as horribly handsome as Kyle Salinas.

CHAPTER NINE

I had my first wet-dream at eighteen. It coincided with my intuitive realization that I was possibly more attracted to men than to women.

In all of my erotic dreams, then, and since, I'm having sex with a man. Sometimes I know the guy, although he's more often than not just a casual acquaintance, or someone merely spotted in passing and whom I thought, at the time, was exceptionally good-looking. I've never had a wet-dream involving a woman or any close male friend. I've had exactly one dream about Harold, and it was a nightmare. I'm still trying to figure out its Freudian implications.

Frankly, I'm surprised, even in my present dream-state — wherein I seem to know I'm dreaming — that my companion, in this instance, is a quite horny, quite naked, Kyle Salinas. By the way, in most my dreams, erotic or otherwise, I'm often able to stand back, and make clever little "asides." In this dream, I've already observed to myself how great Kyle, as I've always suspected, looks stripped bare.

"Why the fuck am I dreaming of you, of all people?" I come right out and ask him.

"Who else is there around here worth fantasizing about?" he answers. "My half-brother?" He rolls his eyes. "Speaking of sex, are you finally going to let me fuck your sexy ass, or not?"

"I don't know … yet." I'm telling myself that sex with Kyle in a dream is probably the best — if not the only — way to have sex with him and not get our fucking all cluttered with bullshit reality. A come is a come is a come, whether in real life or in a dream, so why deprive myself of one, now, when it won't likely ever happen when I'm awake, especially since Dreamland sex comes unhampered by emotional baggage, or by fears of venereal disease, or by worries as to whether or not Kyle's cock will or won't split my virgin asshole from my backbone to my balls?

"Okay," I say. "Why not? I'm tired of it being virgin."

"Jesus H. Christ!" he says. "Your asshole is virgin? No way am I going to be the one to pop its cherry."

"Don't be silly," I cajole. Now that I've decided to do the deed with him, the idea that he's going to leave me high and dry is more than a little disappointing.

"Sorry, buddy," he says and starts to get dressed.

"Fuck!" I say loud enough to wake me.

I'm disoriented, it takes me awhile to realize why I'm sprawled naked, atop my sheets, my hard dick in my hand, my fingers drooled with so much pre-cum that the overflow fills my navel.

I'm just beginning a fast-and-furious pump of my meat - probably better than anything Kyle can provide, anyway - when there's audible scratching (Dracula?) at my door.

I grab bed clothes and pile them atop my swollen dick — behold, a virtual Mt. Everest! — by way of hoped-for disguise.

"Yes?"

The doorknob turns, the door squeaks open a crack.

"Mr. Maltese?"

Crotch-heavy, I stretch for the bedside light.

"Jenny, honey, is that really you?"

I didn't mean to wake you." She comes in and, thank God, this time doesn't pull the door shut behind her; she's an innocent little girl, and I'm a grown man sporting an unseemly raging boner; no matter that my stiffy has nothing to do with her and everything to do with her uncle.

"Are you all right?" I check my wristwatch. It's two a.m.

"I'm fine." She comes over and sits in the chair that adjoins the bed.

"When did you get back, honey?" I'm wondering if Kyle finally managed to run her and her wayward father down.

"About an hour ago."

"Is your daddy with you, honey?" I hope he isn't — if just because Jeremy back sees all of my reasons for remaining at *The Cataracts* suddenly gone.

"He's downstairs with Uncle Kyle." That's that. "We ran out of money." No shit, Sherlock!

"Is your daddy all right?" I wonder how Jeremy is being treated upon his return. I doubt Kyle has killed the fatted calf.

"Dad says he'll keep a stiff upper lip." Jenny examines her small hands for a few seconds. "He sure wasn't keen on coming back."

"Where did you go?"

"To Rome. It was as wonderful as you said."

Her eyelids droop.

"You should probably head off to bed, sweetie," I suggest. "How about we talk more about your little adventure tomorrow?"

"You won't leave without saying good-bye?" Jenny asks. "Uncle Kyle says you're leaving soon."

"I won't leave without saying good-bye." So, Kyle has already announced my departure, what with the return of his half-brother and niece?

Jenny gets up and walks to the door. Before going through it, she turns back.

"You know, you were right," she says. "Daddy doesn't hate me."

"You finally found that out, did you? I'm glad."

"We had a really good time." She disappears into the hall.

After a minute of reflection, my cock having lost its hardness during Jenny's brief visit, I reach for my robe and follow her into the hallway. She's nowhere in sight, but I hear male voices downstairs.

Before I reach the bottom of the stairs, Kyle and Jeremy come out of the library. Both immediately stop talking when they see me.

"William!" Jeremy speaks first. Certainly, he doesn't look any the worse for his absence. He looks downright handsome in white safari jacket, white shirt, white slacks, and white shoes. He leaves Kyle's side and comes to me, saying. "How about a hug for this prodigal son returned to *The Cataracts?*"

He opens his arms. I find it quite natural to walk into them.

He holds me tightly. I respond in kind.

"I'll leave you two to your crotch-grinding," Kyle says, "only hoping that you'll not hatch too many conspiracies in my absence."

Over Jeremy's shoulder, I watch Kyle go.

"He's not too pleased to have me back," Jeremy says. He breaks from me and nods me back toward the library he just exited.

"He seemed anxious enough to have you back once he discovered you were gone," I say and nod assent when Jeremy lifts a decanter of cognac and an eyebrow to ask if I'd like to join him in a drink.

"Kyle would have preferred I left him a few more days alone with you before coming back." Jeremy pours us each a couple fingers of liqueur. "He's rather taken by you, you know?"

"Sure he is!" I reach for the offered glass of expensive booze.

"It's true." Jeremy sips from his glass and motions me toward a couple of chairs. "Even Jenny sees it."

"Jenny seems exceptionally pleased with your little adventure." I don't want to have to spend any time reminding Jeremy how Kyle's chief interest in me is still my percentage of *The Cataracts.* "Am I to understand there's a mending of the father-daughter schism?"

Jeremy sits on one large wing-back chair. I sit on the one across from him.

"Certainly, we have a better rapport, now, than I can ever remember. Whatever was it that you told her?"

"Me?"

His eyebrow arches, and he says, "I suppose, in the end, it makes little difference what you said. I'll just thank you for having said it, and I'll graciously leave it at that."

I indulge a small swallow of cognac

"Jenny and I owe you an apology," he says and cups his snifter so that it's warmed by both palms. "We really didn't think, when we rushed off, that Kyle would suspect you as our accomplice"

I can't bring myself to be angry with Jenny or Jeremy for their had-to-be-obvious-even-at-the-time oversight.

"I hear you saw Rome?" I say.

"Jenny asked if we could go there. I'd never really allowed myself to believe she might like anywhere but here."

"Did you get another sales agreement drawn up while you were up and about?" I glance toward the library door to be sure Kyle isn't hiding in the wings.

"Oh, to be quite frank, William, I've quite accepted that there'll be no outwitting Kyle. I didn't do much of anything, while gone, but sight-see with my daughter. She's as fond of the Villa d' Este as her mother was."

He examines what remains of the contents of his liqueur glass.

"What, I wonder, did Kyle tell you about Jenny's mother and me."He leans back in his chair and eyes me over the edge of his brandy snifter "Kyle's not really the big mean ogre he sometimes appears, and that I sometimes attempt to make him."

Needless to say, I'm surprised by that admission — it seems such an adult thing to say. I've had a hard time looking on Jeremy as anything other than a fun-loving boy who thinks grown-ups are out to deprive him of his well-deserved good times.

"It's always easier to blame someone specific for the rotten way things go, rather than admit it's more likely everyone who's a little to blame," he says.

He finishes his drink and places his empty glass on a nearby coffee table. He pyramids his index fingers so their tips indent the underside of his chin.

"Kyle is easy to condemn, because he's so good at playing feudal lord in the castle. Of course, *The Cataracts*, by rights, should be all his ... would have been his ... if our old man's finances hadn't been flushed down the proverbial toilet. The *Cataracts* and a useless piece of property somewhere off in the wilds of Paraguay were all my father salvaged from his bankruptcy. My part of the original inheritance was suddenly a bunch of worthless scraps of paper. So, dad, trying to be fair, divvied up what little he had left. And who came away thinking he was the wronged son? Why I did, of course. What was my share in *The Cataracts* compared to what I figured I *should* have had? Besides, I hated, and still hate this place."

He casts a covetous glance at the liqueur decanter and reaches for his empty glass. As he gets up, his look inquires whether or not I'm ready for seconds. I shake my head.

He replenishes his glass, brings it back to his chair, and sits back down with it. He takes a large swallow of his drink.

Meanwhile, I'm confirming my earlier opinion that he's a strikingly handsome young man. His aren't the rugged good looks of his half-brother but, rather, more refined. Kyle is a sculpture in the rough. Jeremy is one possibly too-perfect —too much tweaking done.

"International Hotels contacted my father," Jeremy says. "They said they might be interested in the property here in Iguassu. My mother and I pressured Dad to sell. He was naturally reluctant. He felt guilty, of course, about the raw deal he'd be giving Kyle by selling *The Cataracts* out from under him. Kyle was the older son, after all, and the old man had left him, here, for years on end while the rest of us were traipsing around Europe."

He took another swallow of cognac and, immediately, followed it up with another.

"My mother and I plotted. Against my better judgment, and certainly contrary to my sexual preferences, I married poor

Adrienne, and even scrounged up enough cash for a short honeymoon in Italy. The plan was to give dad a grandson. Certainly, he wanted one, perceptively suspicious that neither Kyle nor I would likely ever manage that miracle. No grandson, though, for all of my fucked-Adrienne-with-my-eyes-shut efforts; only Jenny. My poor used and abused young bride of less than one year died in childbirth."

He rolls his liqueur in its container and watches how the thick fluid clings tackily to the inside of the crystal.

"My male-chauvinist father wasn't nearly as thrilled with a granddaughter as he would have been with a grandson."

The smile he gives me takes on a thoroughly mischievous character.

"Of course, suddenly finding out *you* owed a percentage of everything was a ray of light in this man's darkness," he says. "Once again, I found myself hoping to get my ticket out of here, International Hotels having upped their offer after father's death. I even managed to fly to Rio to take up some plotting with them. I came back to *The Cataracts*, able to intercept your letter in reply to Kyle's initial query about selling; I mailed you my offer. When I got word you were on your way here, I arranged for Kyle's Jeep to break down in the middle of nowhere until I could get you to the house and, hopefully, get your signature on all the paperwork. Unfortunately, Kyle wouldn't stick to the part I'd written for him."

He drains the last of his brandy and, once again, puts the empty glass on the coffee table.

"You're no doubt wondering what brings on this sudden burst of true confession." He rests a forearm and hand regally along each arm of his chair. "Other, of course, than the old saw that confession is supposedly good for the soul. The fact being that I merely have finally accepted the fact that my chances for escape from here have run their course. Like it or not, I'm stuck here. So, I've decided to give up the fight or, *flight*, surrender unconditionally, and end my days here, in a blissful alcoholic stupor, much as my dear mother did when she was suddenly forced to realize there was no real escape for her, either."

"For heaven sake, Jeremy, you're acting as if your life is over. You're only in your twenties. If you don't like it here, what's to prevent you from going elsewhere and getting a job? You might not end up as rich as Midas, but you can certainly make enough to support you and Jenny."

"Doing what, do you think?" he asks.

"You're young, you're in exceptionally good health. There must be any number of things you can do."

"Digging ditches?" His facetiousness is evident.

"A stint of doing manual labor might do you a world of good." I'm not kidding, either.

"Let's *do* get real, William!" He leans toward me. "There's a whole army of Third-World people out there ready and willing to do all of the world's ditch-digging. I'm not qualified to do that or anything else. I was raised to be a rich wastrel, and a wastrel is what I remain, albeit no longer rich, and that's what I'm likely to keep on being — ad infinitum. Kyle has the advantage of knowing the ropes, as regards the farming of this place, but me …? Even if the role of gentleman farmer ever could become my cup of tea…?"

"You simply can't spend your next sixty or seventy years sucked to the opened end of a liquor bottle."

"Oh, I doubt there are sixty or seventy years left in me."

"You'd be surprised how long some alcoholics last." I've known a few.

"There's always the balcony as a way out." He gives me a crooked smile.

"Don't even fucking suggest something so absurd!" I stand and slop what's left of my cognac over the back of my hand.

"Trouble?"

Jeremy and I turn simultaneously to see Kyle in the doorway.

Jeremy comes to his feet. "I was just going to bed and had suggested William might like to join me. Probably a good thing he declined, because I'm beginning to feel a bit jet-lagged from my flight in and would probably be a rotten fuck." He gives me a slight bow. "If you'll both excuse me…?"

I have plenty more to say, but I doubt it can effectively be said with Kyle in the room.

Jeremy nods to his brother and walks past him and on out.

"He's really not pleased to be back, is he?" Kyle says, strolling over to the liqueur decanter that was far fuller before Jeremy and I had at it. He doesn't pour himself a drink, though, but merely rolls the cut-glass container between his hands.

"I'd say that was the understatement of this year and possibly next," I say, place my empty glass on the nearby coffee table, and lick spilled cognac from the back of my hand.

"Had a few drinks, did he?" Kyle asks, his fingers lingering on the decanter.

"Only a couple." So easily, I come to Jeremy's defense.

"He's drunk, you know," Kyle says, leaving the liqueur and walking to a position nearer to where I'm standing.

"On two drinks of cognac?" It could happen, but it doesn't seem likely.

"He was drinking on the plane," Kyle says. "A lot."

"He didn't *act* drunk." I wonder if Kyle isn't simply out to downgrade his brother — yet again.

"Just because he's not sloppy drunk doesn't mean he's not drunk," Kyle says.

"Maybe," I reluctantly admit.

"If there was anything I could do for Jeremy's peace of mind, don't you think I'd do it?" Kyle asks.

"Except sell *The Cataracts*," I say. It isn't a question.

"Do you really think you're being fair to throw that alternative in my face?" he asks. He looks downtrodden. I feel guilty.

"Yes, maybe, I am being unfair," I admit. "It's just that it's not pleasant for me to see what's happening here."

Kyle closes the remaining distance between us. He puts his hands on my shoulders. When I purposely don't look at him, he uses his right hand to force me into doing so.

"There is nothing you, or Jenny, or I, can do to help Jeremy," he says. "There's no one who can help Jeremy but Jeremy."

CHAPTER TEN

It's a gamble, to be sure, in Harold's agency taking on Jeremy as a model. Even if that can help me determine, once and for all, if Kyle's interest in me *really* extends beyond my percentage of *The Cataracts*. If not for Harold's support, good guy and good friend that he's turned out to be, I wouldn't likely have seen the possibility that was there for the seeing.

"If it works out, it works out," Harold says. "If it doesn't work out, you simply come back to London and lick your wounds, or let me lick them for you. It's not going to do you any good to spend the rest of your life wondering how it *might* have been."

However, Jeremy doesn't see it as workable. "Kyle won't let me go," he says. "He'll be fearful that you and I will meet up, away from *The Cataracts*, and do what he's so far kept us from doing. Certainly, you aren't prepared to stay on here, by way of collateral, for as long as it takes me to prove myself as a model."

"How about if I just go ahead and sign over my percentage of *The Cataracts* to Kyle, here and now, giving him no reason to keep hold onto either of us?" I plunge right on in.

"He couldn't pay you what your share is worth." Does Jeremy still hold out hope of pulling off a coup d'etat?

"I'll take whatever he offers," I say. "God knows, whatever I get will be more than I ever originally expected."

"What possibly makes you think I can make it as a model in your friend's agency?" He looks toward the liquor cabinet but doesn't make any move in that direction.

"Harold and I work in the modeling business," I remind. "We've seen the types who succeed. You have the look." I should have seen that sooner. Thank God Harold is always scouting for new talent.

"And if you're both wrong?"

"What have you to lose? If you fail, you fail. You can still come back here and drink yourself into oblivion. Kyle will still feel too guilty to kick you and Jenny out, even if and when he controls the majority.

"What about Jenny?"

"She'll be safe enough, and happy enough, here, until you get settled enough to send for her."

"You sure *you*, personally, want to risk this?" he asks.

"What possible risk is there for me?" Who am I kidding?

"Excuse me if I have this wrong," Jeremy apparently has no qualms about spelling it out, "but I suspect you love my half-brother. I suspect he may even love you, but, what if he doesn't? What if it's only *The Cataracts* he's really ever wanted from your relationship?"

I shrug. I've considered that and have decided to accept whatever the consequences. Knowing the truth, I keep telling myself, over and over, is always better.

"Do it, then," he says, looking out the window to where the spray from the falls mists up and over the lip of the gorge. "If worse comes to worst, you and I will have each other's shoulders to cry on."

CHAPTER ELEVEN

The legal paperwork is signed and witnessed. Kyle walks the lawyer to the front door.

"I'm going to pack," Jeremy says and leaves me alone in the library.

I should pack, too, and I'm about to get up and do that when Kyle returns.

He locks the door behind him.

"I'm confused," I say.

"I've locked the door not to keep you from leaving but to keep me from turning tail."

I'm more confused and must look it.

"I have this inexplicably desperate need to fuck you, and to be fucked by you — having had it for a very long time, now — and it can no longer be explained by me merely wanting to use sex as a means of getting you to hand over your share of *The Cataracts*," he says. "I've never felt what I'm feeling for anyone before, and that leaves me scared fucking shitless."

"You think you'll ask, once again, for sex, and I'll once again turn you down?"

"Your answer, yes, or no, has very little to do with it," he says. "Whatever you say isn't going to make what I feel go away any time soon."

I'm flattered and made feel-good by his revelation. My fear of his disappearing, now that he's gotten what he wants, by way of my percentage of the house and grounds, is far less than it was just a few seconds before.

While I'd always hoped this moment would come …

"What am I going to do?" he asks. "Any suggestions?"

"How about I tell you that I had a dream about you wherein I agreed to let you fuck me, and you turned me down because I was a virgin?"

He laughs.

"Fat chance that would ever happen in real life," he says and adjusts his obviously hard cock, ill-concealed by his trousers. Suddenly - an epiphany? -his demeanor changes. "You're not a virgin, are you?"

"Well, I've fucked a few women in my time. As for men, I've been saving myself for Mr. Right." I'm still not sure just when it was decided for me — by karma, fate, or kismet — that Kyle Salinas was the man I wanted to tear my illusionary man-hymen.

"Jesus!" Then, he repeats himself, only louder.

His hand is back on his bulged crotch. His cock leaks pre-cum so profusely that a damp spot appears on the outside-from-the-inside of his trousers. My cock additionally webs with pre-cum the crotch of my underpants

"I'm not just talking sex, here, by the way," he says.

"I'm not, either, if it comes to that," I say. "Think we should take this opportunity, though, to better define whatever *it* is?"

"Can I fuck you?" If he sounds tentative, and he does, it's likely because of my having turned him down so many times that he doesn't really believe his good luck, this time around.

"I think it's time." No going back for me, now.

"Actually, I think you should fuck me first," he offers in alternative.

Unexpected as his suggestion is, it makes my hard cock dance in my pants and leak a whole new river of goo.

"I think we should do *it* on the balcony." He begins to disrobe. Quickly, I follow suit.

Finished first, looking very Greek God-like, even with hair on his chest and belly, he slides open the door to the balcony and steps out into the roars from the gorge. I follow after.

The fine mist that tickles my nakedness is more sexual stimulant than coolant. Or, maybe, I'm so horny I could stand directly under the main Iguassu falls and still be hot to trot.

Kyle leans against the balustrade and momentarily peers into the pit below.

"Jesus, be careful!" My mind's-eye is simultaneously filled with the wonder of his naked body and with the definite attending possibilities for cruel fate to punctuate this moment of expectation with a collapse of the railing and my intended deflowerer's tumble into wet oblivion.

"We have a structural engineer in every year to check the viability of all overlooks," he assures, his voice muffled by the roar. "The railing will support me, and it will support you fucking me from the rear."

His hands reach back, take hold of his ass, and open his buttocks along his steamy crack. There's a thin line of damp black hair from his backbone to his balls.

The opening of his asshole looks way to small to take on my cock.

"Having second thoughts?" he asks. "How about I promise you a ride like none you've ever had while fucking pussy? In fact, after you've fucked my butt, I can pretty much guarantee you won't ever be going back to snatch. Nor are you ever going to want any other man's asshole but mine."

Certainly, at this moment, *his* asshole has my undivided attention.

"Fuck me," he says. "If you want me to beg, I can do that."

"No need to beg, unless that turns you on," I say, up close behind his behind. The uplifted length of my dick squeezes, like a wiener in a bun, into the vertical crease of his ass. My belly and chest spoon his butt and back.

He turns his head over one shoulder to kiss me, and then he returns his gaze to the gorge. I see the watery turmoil over his shoulder and down below. I don't know if it's the view of him or the roiling water that makes me dizzy.

I pull back my lower body far enough to insert my right hand between us and take hold of my cock to lower it, drawbridge like, into the space between my crotch and his asshole.

Slick with pre-cum, my cockhead slides into position against the pliant softness of his winked pucker. He sighs.

"Stick me, please," he says and provides a rear-buck that immediately puts the first inch of my dick inside him.

If I have initial intentions of going slow and easy, a primitive part of my brain takes complete control and demands that I throw caution to the wind and stick him hard and fast.

Actually, I'm surprised by how quickly, how easily, and how fully his butt swallows my whole dick. My belly hits his ass — hard — with a loud slap. My scrotum swings forward and up and whacks, painfully but pleasurably, the overhang of his asscheeks.

"Oh, sweet Jesus!" I moan loudly against his shoulder. My hands slide his torso, through the hair on his belly and chest. My palms flatten over his taut nipples.

His asshole clamps vise-like around my plugging dick. I wonder if I can pull out my boner even if I try.

Am I surprised when, suddenly, I'm prematurely, by my way of figuring, teetering on the brink of orgasm, having achieved nothing more than the slotting of my dick up Kyle's tight ass? Damned right I'm surprised! I've fucked some cunt dry before finally getting off. That I've come so far, so fast — during this butt-fuck of this man just begun — is as embarrassing and disappointing as it is wondrous.

"Sorry," I whisper against his neck.

The orgasmic shudders that take hold and shake the entire length and breadth of me are unbelievably intense; like nothing I've ever experienced. It seems as if all of me suddenly funnels to my dick for jettisoning up Kyle's asshole.

My prick force-feeds Kyle's asshole more cum than I imagine my testicles capable of producing. Spunk erupts in greater and greater gushes.

"Oh, buddy, yes!" he says. His hands reach behind us to hard-clamp to my ass … pulling me on in … closer … closer … closer to him … until we seem one and the same creature.

My knees buckle. My full weight collapses against him. If the balcony is going to fail, it'll be now.

"Wish I could have made it longer and better for you," I finally, breathlessly, apologize.

"It's quality time that counts, buddy," he says. "It was good for me, believe me."

"Still, I think I need lessons from a master. Do I hear you volunteer?"

"Lesson one, Grasshopper: the fastest way to keep your cock from going soft after fucking ass is quickly getting your own ass fucked."

"Sounds like a plan."

"Though, taking into account your butt is virgin, its fuck might best be performed with me down on my back and you sitting on my cock at your leisure."

"Color me horse on a merry-go-round-pole ready."

"Pull your cock from my ass whenever you're ready, then, but don't hurry on my account."

As much as I've blasted into him, I'm surprised my dick hasn't gone soft. So solid does it remain, though, that I'm tempted to fuck his ass far better a second time. That said, I'm more enticed by the idea of my virgin rear end *finally* jabbed by an experienced pecker so much more ready, willing, and able to do so than it had been in Dreamland.

My dick un-slots, suctioning a mess of my pearly spent cream out with it to drool the insides of Kyle's thighs.

He turns toward me and smiles. His cock is so hard and impressive that I can't believe my asshole will ever successfully take it, no matter how anxious he is to fuck me, and no matter how eager I am to have it him do it. No matter that Kyle's seemingly equally small asshole has taken my big cock with no resulting harm done.

"My butt is suddenly very cock-hungry," I say.

Our bodies are glossy with our sweat and with condensed mist from the falls.

I figure Kyle will lie in the chaise longue, but he sinks to the balcony, instead. He lies on his back, his knees bent, his thighs providing the slide way along which my back can glide to dump my dick eventually on and over his dick — from his cock corona to his cock base.

I straddle his supine body, as if I'm the Colossus and he's the harbor of Rhodes. My legs slowly buckle, and my knees go to either side of his chest. The balcony floor is hard, but the only hardness with which I'm really concerned is what juts impressively from Kyle's crotch.

"Okay, my sexy greenhorn, let the ride begin," he says. His one hand pulls his horse-dick to an aim-for-the-sky position, his pre-cum wet cockhead is suddenly ready and waiting for my asshole to make its descent over it.

As horny as Kyle must be — my cock, when previously fucked up his asshole and blasting, not having provided him enough stimulation for his own eruption — he doesn't try to hurry me. His, "Just take your own sweet time, cowboy," makes me happy as hell that my first time isn't with someone as naïve at man-man sex as I am.

I reach behind and below my ass and find his hand-wrapping-his-cock. My ass lowers until I feel his cock's wet corona within the beginning fold of my asscrack. I slightly realign my butt over his erection and sit farther. My hand on his hand-on-his-cock pulls his bulky cockhead to my target area.

The knob of his prick is like a giant fist poised at the entrance to my asshole. No doubt, it's way too big ever to go farther than it already has without doing a good deal of physical damage.

Decision time has arrived. Do I risk my ass split from stem to stern by Kyle's monster dick, inviting debilitating infection in a tropical environment where an itched mosquito bite can turn life-threatening overnight, or do I go ahead and experience what I've been long wanting to experience with some man-cock, in general ... lately, with Kyle's cock, specifically ?

I allow more of my weight to concentrate atop his at-the-ready cockhead. My anal pucker concaves but doesn't open. I sit deeper. Like a camera lens, my sphincter begins to open ... open ... sweet Jesus! ... open ...

I pause. His cockhead isn't even totally up my butt, but I'm feeling as if I'm sitting with a wedge about to split me. Truly, I wonder if this is going to happen, or if I'm going to chicken out. Only my memory of how my big dick managed its successful slide up Kyle's, seemingly as small as mine, asshole, keeps me from getting up, getting dressed, getting the hell out of here.

I want this, I tell myself. Quit being such a fucking pussy and get on with it.

"No need to rush," Kyle reassures. "We've lots of time."

Maybe, if he'd just rapidly lift his hips and jab his dick inside of me, I wouldn't be so concerned with the daunting anticipation of having his prick fucked any deeper.

My rectum has just enough grip on the tip of his dick so that I don't need my hand any longer on his hand-on-his-cock. Both of my hands, palms flat, go dead-center on his muscled chest; my fingers burrow his chest hair and hard-grip his pectoral muscles.

I look into his handsome face. His purple eyes are slightly glazed but cognizant. His smile dimples his cheek.

I kiss the cleft of his chin and purposely sit myself an additional inch over his still-many-inches-to-go penis.

"Jesus!" I say.

"Little bounces will spread the goo," he says. "My pre-cum can lubricate as it goes."

Wanting this to work, I do as instructed. My ass lifts along his cock but not so far as to free it. My rectum returns along a path made smoother and slicker by the natural lubricant his leaking prick put there. I force-feed my butt an additional inch of his dick ... pause ... raise ... repeat ... repeat ...

Although I once thought it quite impossible for my ass to swallow his big prick, I'm being proved wrong. Each rise and fall of my rectum over his cock allows for a deeper downslide.

When his entering dick pokes my prostate, I groan, and a sudden gush of pre-cum leaks my dick and his. My cock, by the way, is so fucking hard by now that a casual observer would never know it had, just minutes before, erupted all my nuts had to offer at the time.

"Oh, fuck … oh, fuck," Kyle says appreciatively. For the first time, he loses a bit of his self-control, in that his hips reflexively jerk in a successful attempt to put more of him inside me.

My butt is so adjusted to what's happening, although I still experience a decided sense of being filled to capacity, there's no real discomfort or pain.

"Fucking damn, I want your whole prick inside of me!" I sit harder and deeper to make it happen. My butt drops almost, but not quite, into a complete sit of his pelvic saddle.

My hands, still anchored to his hairy chest, push me back to align my back along his lifted thighs as my butt finally advantages a successful completion of its descent.

"Ohhhh, mother of God!" My voice is breathless.

My head rocks back on my neck to put my Adam's apple into high relief.

Sweat, previously pooled in my jugular notch, along with condensed mist from the cataracts, commences a slow trickle through my pectoral cleavage.

My left hand drops between my legs and finds my compacting scrotum. I roll my balls, one against the other.

His dick expands and contracts up my butt.

"Oh, cowboy, this was so worth the wait!" he says. I agree.

Thank God, I hadn't chickened out before braving it to this point, I so completely stuck and pleasure-filled. Ecstasy sunbursts my cock-plugged asshole into the rest of my body.

Where there was a time I thought I could be content with just the successful slide of my ass over Kyle's dick, thanking my lucky stars if I could just manage that, I'm now intuitively more inclined to take full advantage and milk the experience for all it's worth.

I slide up his thighs, and my asshole leaves his exiting slick dick behind. When I've raised to where only his cockhead remains inside of me, its flare firmly gripped by the rubber-band squeeze of my sphincter, I put all of my weight into a return trip to again have my ass cupped by his crotch. His dick is, once again, stuffed completely inside me.

"Sweet, virgin, ass!" His head rocks and rolls. His eyes are wide. His mouth is open. His tongue flicks. His hands take hold of my thighs, first firm, then harder, as I begin another up-slide.

"Virgin ass no longer," I tell him and thank God for the wonders his cock performs.

"Oh, cowboy," he says. Obviously, he's having a good time. Whether it's as good a time as I'm having is debatable, because I'm having one helluva good time. In fact, I'm enjoying so much that I simultaneously bemoan how I've waited so damned long to let it happen. Except, possibly, it wouldn't have been nearly as good, with or without Kyle, had it happened any sooner. There's something to be said for the right time, the right place, the right man, the right way.

I'm feeling really good, all trace of discomfort long gone. There's only pleasure derived from each additional slip and slide of his dick in and out of my rectum.

"Fuck your ass ... fuck your ass ... fuck you!" Kyle chants.

Continually, my ass takes his prick and lets mostly go of it. Swallows. Disgorges to cocktip. Gobbles and spits ... gobbles and spits ...

I'm really into this fuck. I'm flying high. I can't bounce hard enough, fast enough.

When Kyle grabs my hard and leaking dick, using it as a handle to push and pull my lower body down and up over his cock, I know my virgin-no-longer ass, and my first-time-jacked-by-another man cock, aren't going to need much more humping and pumping to push me over the orgasmic edge. No matter that my balls have already deposited one hearty load — up Kyle's ass, my testicles are definitely primed for an encore.

"Jesus, fuck!" I sit Kyle's stud cock one final time with an accompanying torque of my ass that twists my prostate against his swollen prick.

I fall forward; my hands flatten over his nipples that are tack-like and dig into my palms.

My back arches, my ass burrows. I want more of him inside me, eager to sit even deeper in his lap, even though there's no more of him to be had.

His cum squirts deep inside of me and triggers my own eruption of hot-and-heavy sperm. My dick squirts its heavy cream like a heavy-duty fire-hose dispensing pressurized water. Great bulbous comets, with long tails, are launched, caught by gravity, and eventually plopped in wet-lattice designs from Kyle's belly to his face.

"Sweet Jesus!" we sing in two-part harmony.

The last of his hearty pulses of cum up my ass, my cock still squirting, I fall completely over my lover, my belly to his belly, my chest to his chest.

I lick my cum from the corner of his mouth and taste his essence and mine.

"I love your ass, and I love you," he says when my lips against his release enough pressure to allow him to say anything.

"I love your cock and love you, too," I put words to the miracle.

My ass clamps down hard to wring his still-submerged pecker of the very last of his deliciously pleasurable man-spunk.

EPILOGUE

Kyle is my first and only man. He is my friend and my only lover — for fifty wonderful years.

When he dies of a snake bite, I bury him on a knoll overlooking his beloved *The Cataracts* and Iguassu falls.

Jeremy, by now with a long history as a successful model and his own modeling agency just launched — and Jenny, a marine biologist with a very handsome and charming husband and four children — attend the funeral but don't stay on afterwards.

I stay on, though. Every month or so, I field another lucrative offer from another hotel chain to take *The Cataracts* off my hands.

I don't intend to sell. I intend to spend my remaining days, sitting on this balcony, overlooking this gorge, biding my time until I'm once again re-united with the one true love of my life.

WET
DREAMS

LAURA BAUMBACH

As he walks into the bedroom I shift under the blankets, letting him know I'm still awake, easing from my side to my back. Lately, our schedules have conflicted and private time, intimate time, time to take pleasure in each other, has become next to nonexistent.

Extended time together as a couple requires effort. We need to synchronize our calendars, watches and libidos. Until then, I'll take a stolen moment in the middle of the night, if he's willing. I know he's always able.

He lies down on his side of the bed and adjusts the pillows and blankets the way he likes them. I feel a twinge of disappointment at that. He's getting ready to go to sleep, my subtle offer ignored or missed. He settles into his customary sleeping position, flat on his back, remaining still for several minutes. Disappointed, I roll back over to my side, my back facing him.

I could just tell him what I want, but I don't want to try enticing him if he's too tired. Neither of us ends up enjoying ourselves then and that's more disappointing than never having made the effort to begin with. Maybe I'll have a nice, sticky dream to ease my disappointment.

Then a snap-click breaks the silence. A large, warm hand reaches across the distance between us, settling on my back, rubbing at the base of my neck. The touch is unusually warm, wet and inviting. I recognize immediately that he has covered his hands with a warming gel, its slippery consistency so silky wet and delightfully warm.

I relax into his touch, letting him know I'm enjoying it, that it's welcome. He moves closer and presses his body up next to mine, spooning behind me, pulling me nearer. One hand glides beneath over my chest and a thumb strums over a nipple, bringing it to life, hard and erect and wanting.

His other hand brushes away the hair at the side of my neck, clearing a spot for him to taste the tender skin behind my ear. Wet lips and tongue mouth the flesh, lapping and sucking until I'm squirming.

Torn between the sharp tingling of pleasure in my breast and the wet, nuzzling sweetness at my neck, I'm not sure which to encourage more of. Without my realizing it, my hips start to push back against him, the rest of my body demanding attention as well.

He switches nipples, all the while kissing a wet trail down my shoulder. By the time he makes it to my arm, he is silently urging me to turn towards him, pushing the considerable weight of his larger body over onto me. I shift onto my back, and his legs entwine with mine, pinning me to the bed.

Sharp, almost painful rays of pleasure burst from my left nipple as he laps at it with his broad tongue, the rough texture sensitizing and teasing the taut flesh before he sucks it through pursed lips to rest between his teeth. After a few introductory nibbles that make me tremble and moan, he settles down to his favorite form of foreplay—nursing at my teats until they are hard and full, swollen, wet, aching. Low moans of delight escape me and fill the air, mixing with the sweet, wet slurps of his suckling.

The moist sounds heighten my desire, letting me imagine that he is actually nursing, drinking from me, devouring me. The image is erotic. The desire to have him inside me magnifies.

I'm finding it difficult to lie still, but his legs hold me tight, the arm across my abdomen weighing me down. I run my hand over his shoulders and head, seeking out a way to return the pleasure, but I'm unable to touch most of his body. He likes it that way in the beginning, likes to lavish all the attention on me, focusing on my pleasure, my desires, my needs, to bring me to the point of being a writhing, needful, wanton creature. After all this time, he hasn't lost his touch. I'm nearly there.

His right hand massages the flesh around the nipple in his mouth while his left hand pinches and tweaks the other. Knowing it's time to increase the tempo, he trails his left hand down my stomach and combs his fingers through the soft curls surrounding my dick. His knee nudges my thighs wider and he settles the weight of his leg on mine, pinning it in place, shifting his body to rest between my legs.

His hand brushes over my hot flesh, stroking and petting. He briefly toys with my balls, making them tighten, then moves to tease the swollen head of my cock; the light, stroking touch of his fingertips making me arch up to find more. My skin is overly warm where the gel has touched, wet and slick;, the rest of my body cool in the night air.

The sucking at my breast becomes nibbles, teeth scraping over the tip, working the flesh to a point of raw delight. Every sharp sting, every swipe of his rough tongue, sends thrills down my body that meet at the point where his fingers are stroking me. A buzzing need simmers in my belly, deep inside, behind my leaking dick. I'm about to beg him to take me when the fingers leave my shaft only to return a moment later, slick and cool, to circle the tight ring of my asshole, teasing and soothing me all at once.

His lips at my nipple vanish and my lips are taken instead. I gasp at the sudden change, allowing his tongue to snake in to lap at the ridged lining of my mouth. I twirl my tongue around his, sucking and stroking, silently encouraging. The only sound he likes to hear during our lovemaking is our own gasps and grunts.

I open my mouth wider, intent on drawing his tongue in deeper, when I feel wet fingers, now slick and cool, glide over the flesh of my ass. Knowing what to expect, I open my legs wider and relax into the kiss and he becomes ravenous for my lips and tongue. Surging up over me, he plunders my mouth, sucking on my tongue and stroking the sensitive tissue of my palate. His lubed fingers mimic his tongue, both digits rubbing over my ass before they ease inside.

I'm overwhelmed with sensory input. My nipples ache, hard and raw, straining to regain some kind of attention. My mouth is swollen and bruised, surrendering to the eager assault by his tongue, first broad and gentle, then stiff and plundering. His fingers set me on fire, their sweet rhythm of twisting and thrusting up my ass sending shivers of lust and need to every cell, until even my scalp tingles with the heat of desire.

Abruptly pulling away, he scrambles to move between my trembling knees, forcing my hips up onto his bent thighs in one swift, aggressive motion. One hand massages my chest, alternating nipples, pinching and strumming them while his other hand is busy dribbling more lube from the bedside stand onto his rigid, straining shaft. I reach down and link my fingers with his around his cock, give him a few firm strokes to work the fluid over his hard flesh, pulling a groan from deep inside his chest.

Lifting my hips higher, he moves in closer. He takes my hands away and places them on my breasts, murmuring, "Play with your tits. I want to watch."

I finger and pull at them, twisting them and flicking at them until the raw sharpness returns. They feel heavy and thick, the dark skin crinkled in tight grooves, the flesh burning, the tips glistening with his salvia. More groans escape me and I close my eyes. I lick my lips, trying to recapture the feel and taste of his tongue down my throat.

A fresh stabbing burn pulls my focus back and I open my eyes to look at him as he enters me. He is caught in the fine torture of working his shaft into the tight heat of my ass, a liquid fire bathing him, caressing him, opening to him. His head is tilted back, face contorted, the grimace of pleasure so intense it looks painful. His hands grip my hips and with a measured lunge he pulls me to him, thrusting forward, impaling me fully.

Wrapping my legs around him, I slide one hand under me to stroke his balls that are wedged tightly against my ass cheeks, but he's too close to climax to tolerate my touch. He moves my hand to my crotch, layering his fingers over mine as he moves them around my dick, a rapid stroking until I'm gasping and moaning in time to the rhythm. His hand slips away to massage my ass cheeks, allowing him to sink a few millimeters deeper.

Slowly at first, then building to a demanding rhythm, he is thrusting into me harder. The burn builds, then fades away to become a pleasurable ache. I feel full, invaded, possessed. He buries himself deeper and deeper, each pounding thrust harder and harder until he touches that undefined part of me that spasms with each thrust of his cock.

Buried in the very center of my body, he is claiming me, marking me, making me his and his alone. He is so deep inside of me I feel I should be able to taste him when he comes.

And I do taste him. But it is the taste of his skin as he leans down to slip two fingers into my mouth. Imagining his full cock, I suck and lave at them, coating them with salvia and then sucking them dry, pulling them in to bob up and down their length. My tongue teases the underside of the callused pads of his thick fingertips, pretending they're the head of his engorged cock.

His thrusts quicken and it's too much for me. I suck hard on the fingers in my mouth, careful not to bite down. I love the feeling of being wrapped in moisture—wetness of my mouth around his fingers, the pooling of sweat, both his and mine, in the notch of my neck, the sweet cum leaking from my cock, the slip-slide of lube and his pre-cum coating the walls inside my ass. A true 'wet' dream!

My whole body spasms with the force of my orgasm. Heat explodes from the center of my body and travels out, setting my nipples afire, flushing my skin and clamping down the muscles in my ass to embrace and reclaim my long time lover. I fall into a haze of pleasure, my body tingling with an overload of sensation.

He pulls his hand away from my mouth to grip my hips again, increasing the power of his strokes. They become ragged and uncoordinated. Suddenly, I'm filled with an intense heat, the pulsing of his cock registering against the sensitive tissue he's buried in. His eyes are shut, breath held, and body frozen in place, riding out the storm of his passion.

He slowly relaxes, lowering his chest down to rest on mine, pushing me deeper into the mattress, blanketing me with his hot, sweaty flesh. A quick kiss on the lips, then he turns my head to nuzzle at the salty skin of my neck before sliding out and off to rest beside me. He trails one callused fingertip over a too sensitive nipple just to hear me gasp. Sitting up, he leans over me. By the light of the hallway, I can see the satisfied smile on his face.

Before I can speak, he runs a rough lick of his tongue over the same startled nipple, then drops a kiss in my hair, and a roughly murmured, "Love you" is whispered near my ear.

I run my hand down his chest, letting it rest over his heart before I answer with a contented, sleepy, "Love you, too."

Lovemaking always energizes him, so I'm not offended when he turns away, bouncing out of the bed and out of the room. I know he'll go watch television for awhile or wander the house until sleep beckons to him again. If I'm still awake I might be tempted to drop another subtle hint when he comes back to bed. In my book, a man can never have too many wet dreams, especially while awake.

SOUTH OF THE BORDER

LAURA BAUMBACH

This short story, first published in 2007, was the inspiration for the **CRIMES & COCKTAILS** Series. Portions of the story as you read it here don't fit the story line that evolved when the series became a collaboration with mystery writer Josh Lanyon, but it's still a hot tale of wet fun. An expanded, modified version of it will be incorporated into the second book in the series, **TEQUILA SUNRISE**. If you want to taste the full passion of the men in this series pick up a copy of book #1, **MEXICAN HEAT**, a 2009 Lambda Literary Award Finalist as of the printing of this anthology.

Book #2, TEQUILA SUNRISE is due out late 2009.

Gabriel eased down into the large hot tub, letting his sore body adjust to the sizzling heat. He inhaled and the scented steam rose up, invading his nostrils and his mind. The heavy tropical fragrance called up recent memories of late nights on sandy beaches surrounded by exotic flowers and pounding surf. The sand wasn't the only thing getting a pounding the last three nights.

He wiggled his butt on the hard wooden seat, awakening a dull throb that resulted from those memories. Sighing at the satisfied feeling the ache gave him, Gabriel relaxed and leaned back against the tub's sides. His eyes were closed and he let his arms float just under the water's surface. Scooting his butt forward, he splayed his legs to let the soothing heat reach every submerged body part. He flexed his legs slightly, enjoying the gentle tug and pull of the swirling, fluid warmth over his open groin.

Unfazed by displaying his nude body as only the blind can be, Gabriel had shed his clothes in the adjoining bedroom. Then walked through the hotel suite and out to the private courtyard and the waiting tub completely naked. His clothing was in the bedroom, but a handgun was never far from his reach.

The San Francisco Police Department could make him retire after his blinding, but they couldn't take away years of undercover training, a finely honed sense of self-preservation and a ton of bad habits. Years undercover had earned him a whole lot of enemies that weren't going to go away just because he couldn't see them anymore.

The bag of doctored heroin that exploded in his face during his last case left Gabriel Sandalini terribly vulnerable. It took away his sight and a lot of his independence, both for good. But it also gave him two things—a renewed sense of what he wanted from life and someone special to share it with.

The soft sound of cloth rustling captured Gabriel's attention and he smiled as the water rolled and swayed with the addition of another body, a large body by the rise in the water level and the force of the waves. He stayed perfectly still and let the new arrival come to him.

A large, warm mass of firm muscle and sinewy flesh flowed in between his legs and lodged itself tightly against his sprawled lower half. He identified the familiar scent of sweat and coconut oil milliseconds before two callused hands slid up his arms, over his shoulders and around his neck. Once there, strong fingers kneaded and rubbed the tightly knotted muscles at the base of his skull.

"Umm. God, Tony, that feels great." Gabriel sighed and melted into the greedy fingertips. "Uh, Christ, that's good." He rolled his head and let his chin length black hair fall down over his bowed face. He groaned and shifted his groin closer to Antonio's. "God, yeah, right there." Arching his neck until it cracked, he let his head loll back to rest on the edge of the tub. He pushed his hips firmly against the other man's growing erection and wiggled his ass to encourage the swell.

"You're tired." The fingertips moved to caress Gabriel's high cheekbones, then strayed down to stroke gently at his lips. The low, rich tones of Antonio's Spanish accent rolled off his cultured tongue like honey dripping off one of the sun-baked tin roofs that dotted the hillsides on the fringes of town.

Just the sound of the Spaniard's voice made Gabriel's cock swell and his spine tingle, like it had the first time he heard it two years ago.

"I'm not that tired." Gabriel wrapped his legs around Antonio's nude body and hissed at the pleasurable sensation of the hot water swirling around their touching cocks. "Don't think I've ever been *that* tired." He mumbled the word into Antonio's mouth before darting his tongue down the man's throat.

Grabbing a handful of soft dark hair, Antonio forced Gabriel's head back and down, taking control of the ardent kiss. His thickly muscled arms pulled Gabriel farther off the seat, drawing the smaller man's hips forward until they barely rested on the hard surface.

Clamping Gabriel's writhing, clutching body hard against his chest without releasing his hold on Gabriel's hair, Antonio slid one hand under the water, down a firm butt cheek and along the crease that divided his lover's fine ass. His fingers unerringly found the opening to Gabriel's body and he probed and stroked the fluttering muscle, delighting in the low moans of arousal it caused in the other man. Resting the tip of one thick finger just inside Gabriel's ass, Antonio pulled Gabriel back from the kiss by his hair.

Gabriel groaned in frustration and humped his groin into Antonio's, grinding their cocks together. The heated swirling of the hot tub's scented water sent a burst of tropical aroma into the air and the added motion teased at the undersides of their swollen cocks. Gabriel panted and licked his swollen lips.

Sensing the heat of Antonio's face only inches from his, he located the man's mouth by the sound of Antonio's lightly gasped breaths. Surging forward, Gabriel licked the sweat off the man's top lip, savoring the salty-coconut flavor that was Antonio's alone.

"I want you to fuck me," Gabriel grunted and pulled at the other man's lower lip with his teeth, leaving it red and swollen.

"You are always in a hurry, *querido.*" Antonio's talented hand kneaded the scalp under its palm soothingly, his lips laying a path of tiny kisses up Gabriel's arched neck. He interspersed the kisses with an occasional sharp nip, nuzzling his nose into the long, baby fine hair in his hand. "I may not be ready quite yet."

Moving his hands from the big man's back to grip his broad shoulders, Gabriel used the rock hard slabs of muscle and bone to pull his own slender body up and then down, forcing Antonio's cock to slide under his sac and up to his finger-stuffed opening.

"You feel ready to me, bucko." Gabriel bounced on the iron hard shaft resting against his ass, trying to force it inside along with the blunt fingertip. "Come on, man. Make me feel it for a month." He shoved down hard. "It'll help me remember you while you're gone doing that favor for Briggs."

Antonio removed his finger from Gabriel's ass and grabbed both of his lover's squirming hips, stilling them, holding the man immobile. "If you do not want me to go, I will not go, Gabriel." He pressed his lips to Gabriel's ear, his rich, soft Spanish accent rumbling into his lover's damp hair. "You do not need to punish yourself because you cannot go with me." He tightened his grip when Gabriel struggled to free himself, relenting only when the resistance stopped. He tried to keep his tone reasonable. "It is only a few days."

Refusing to talk about anything but sex, Gabriel wormed a hand down between their plastered together bodies and began jerking himself off, setting up a wave of rolling water all around them. "Fine, be a fuckhead then, you ungrateful spick." Despite the biting words, he rested his forehead against Antonio's chin, melting into the big man's bulky frame, his long hair falling down over his sweat streaked face. "If you won't fuck me raw for my sake," he panted, "do it for yourself. Give you something to remember me by."

Sitting back on his heels, Antonio lowered them down farther into the water. "Sometimes you are an incorrigible asshole, my love." He bit Gabriel's ear, then tipped him back against the seat and pulled the smaller man's hips against his groin, balancing Gabriel on the edge of the wooden seat.

"Fine." Gabriel grunted and squirmed, pressing hard on the tip of Antonio's stout cock. "Now get *inside* my asshole and let's do this going away party right." Quivering, Gabriel shoved his face into the crook of Antonio's neck, then whispered in a choked tremble, "I'm done talking about it."

Understanding the underlying, unspoken message of insecurity and fear, Antonio ran a soothing hand down Gabriel's sweaty back, clasped the shaking man tightly to him and whispered into the thick, dark hair under his jaw, "For now, for now."

Rising up, Antonio breached the tight ring of Gabriel's ass with one powerful thrust, gripping his lover's waist to keep him in place. He buried Gabriel's face against his chest, muffling the shout and groan of pained delight from his lover. Wiry legs wrapped around his waist and Antonio concentrated on setting up a rhythm to match Gabriel's frantic humping.

Knowing from long experience of the younger man's need for a forceful, nearly brutal coupling when emotionally upset, Antonio let lose and gave him what he wanted.

Embracing Gabriel's entire body, Antonio slammed into him, dragging Gabriel up his cock to the tip, then slamming him back down to the root of the large shaft. He closed his eyes and focused on the blinding jolts of electric blue pleasure that shot out of his cock and up his spine. "Holy Mother, nothing compares to the feeling of being inside you, Gabriel, nothing. Even like this." Antonio increased the strength of his plunges.

"Pound me senseless, lover. You've only got four of them to beat." The bitterness was still there, but raw lust had smoothed the edges and Antonio could hear the true love and deep affection in Gabriel's voice.

Each thrust forced a sharp grunt from Gabriel, but he gripped Antonio's shoulders in a white-knuckled hold with one hand that refused to weaken as he held on for the ride.

The hot tub's bubbling surface swayed and churned, waves breaking over the sides and baptizing the nearby patio furniture and plants. The scent of tropical flowers became nearly suffocating in intensity.

Antonio opened his eyes to see Gabriel's tightly clenched eyes and arched neck. The younger man's head was thrown back and his body held rigid, meeting each brutal thrust with a grind of his hips. Antonio felt the stirring of orgasm building in the base of his cock and increased the tempo, a hand falling between them to join Gabriel's already frantically stroking palm. He added his own massive fist to the pumping action and felt Gabriel contract the muscles in his ass in response to the added stimulation.

The tight, hot sheath of Gabriel's ass milked his shaft, spasming in a never ending stream of contractions. Feeling the need to come racing past the point of no return, Antonio nuzzled Gabriel's head up and claimed his mouth, swallowing the protest and groans along with Gabriel's tongue. Pulsing into the burning tunnel of heat, Antonio slammed Gabriel down one last time, embedding his cock deep into Gabriel's core, pumping him full of cum at one end and devouring him from the other.

The satiny rod of flesh in his hand jerked and spurted hot milky juice that was washed away as fast as it erupted. Gabriel's erection faded and Antonio forced the fingers of Gabriel's hand to intertwine with his own as the shrinking organ slid from their fingers.

Slowly withdrawing his still half-hard cock from Gabriel's ass, Antonio rubbed over the small of Gabriel's back, soothing and gentling his moody lover. Never releasing Gabriel from the blistering kiss, Antonio rested Gabriel more comfortably on the seat. He eased out of the kiss with a series of soft pecks to Gabriel's bruised mouth, but remained leaning over his exhausted lover, their hands still entwined.

"Better?" His gravelly, soft voice reflected the depth of his understanding of Gabriel's needs. So much so, his question was answered with a whimper from his usually emotionally guarded, iron-willed partner. Taken back by the sound, Antonio smiled in relief when the expected, foulmouthed reply came a heartbeat later.

"Fuck off, asshole. You aren't that good." A small sound that could have been a sniffle made Antonio tip Gabriel's head so he could see Gabriel's expressive face.

"Isn't it time for you to leave yet?" Gabriel muttered.

Antonio smirked at the man's capacity for biting sarcasm. He wrapped his arms around Gabriel's pliant body, enjoying the way the smaller man instantly melted into him, plastering their water-drenched bodies together. He stepped from the tub, maneuvering Gabriel, guiding him where he wanted him to walk. He rubbed his jaw over the side of Gabriel's head resting on his shoulder, moving clumps of wet hair aside to find the small shell of one ear.

He tightened his grip and began walking to their bedroom, mindless of the trail of water they left in their wake. Letting all of the love he had for this amazing, damaged man settle in his voice, Antonio growled softly into the revealed ear, tugging on the tiny lobe with his teeth.

"Not yet, Gabriel. The end of all time has not yet arrived."

ABOUT THE AUTHORS

LAURA BAUMBACH is the award-winning author of numerous short stories, novellas, novels and screenplays. Her favorite genre to work in is manlove or m/m erotic romances. Manlove is not traditional gay fiction, but erotic romances written specifically for the romantic-minded reader, male or female. Married to the same man for almost 30 years, she currently lives with her husband and two sons in the blustery Northeast of the United States but is looking for a warmer location to spend the second half of her professional and family life.

Laura is the owner of ManLoveRomance Press, a small print publishing house that specializes in gay erotic romance, mystery and fiction. (http://www.mlrpress.com) MLR Press was founded in January of 2007. She is also the owner of the promotional co-op for authors of gay romance and fiction, Manloveromance.com. (http://www.manloveromance.com)

You can find Laura on the internet at:
http://www.laurabaumbach.com/
http://groups.yahoo.com/group/laurabaumbachfiction
http://www.mlrpress.com/
http://groups.yahoo.com/group/mlrpress/

WILLIAM MALTESE was born in the Pacific Northwest. He has a BA in Marketing/Advertising. He served a full tour of duty in the U.S. Army and achieved the rank of E-5 before receiving honorable discharge.

He started his literary career by writing for men's pulp magazines. From there, he moved on to pulp novels and, then, into mainstream. He has penned more than 200 books, both fiction and nonfiction, under more than twenty-six pen names. He was a short-list nominee for a Lambda Literary Award for his historical novel (written with Professor Drewey Wayne Gunn), *Ardennian Boy*, and the collection of erotica *Hard Working Men* (with Victor J. Banis, J.P. Bowie and Jardonn Smith). Several of his books have been released in foreign-language editions. He has a long-time listing in *Who's Who in America*.

You can visit his websites at:

www.willimmaltese.com

www.myspace.com/williammaltese

www.myspace.com/draqual

Stimulate yourself.
READ.
www.manloveromance.com
THE HOTTEST M/M EROTIC AUTHORS & WEBSITES ON THE NET